OUT OF THE SHADOW

An Analysis of an Affair

By

Fredericka Heller

To Mary Blake,
Hope you enjoy
this adventure!
Best wishes,
Fredericka

ISBN: 1-4033-3596-6 (e-book)
ISBN: 1-4033-3597-4 (Paperback)

This book is printed on acid free paper.

1stBooks – rev. 09/11/02

I was totally devastated at the end of the affair. At first there was fury from the anger and frustration. I had been betrayed! I felt paralyzed, and at the same time a storm raged inside me. I couldn't think of anything but Neil. I would wake in the middle of the night with the realization that he was gone suddenly sweeping over me and hitting me in the gut. The dreadful feeling of loss returned to end any possibility of more sleep. Vivid thoughts of him constantly churned about in my head. How could he just leave?

Then I went though a period of being obsessed with wanting to know what he was doing. Was he still with the girl? I was afraid of running into him. I was haunted by him, imagining I saw him in the grocery store or a passing car. I began avoiding restaurants and places we had frequented. I fantasized a confrontation and thought of all the things I wanted to say to him, yet knowing I wouldn't have the courage to attack him.

After about six months of agony, my mind started to clear and I slowly began to recover. Now, nearly a year after our breakup, I was over the emotional trauma and desperately trying to comprehend the relationship with the help of my therapist...

PART I

The Green Monkey

Fredericka Heller

CHAPTER ONE

I sat in Byron's small office on the East Side of Santa Fe observing the spindly tropical plant reaching for the window and the two giant moonscape paintings someone had traded for therapy sessions. Byron had been my therapist for many years, and for the past year he had been helping me through my breakup with Neil. I was still dwelling on why he left, going from anger to depression to tears to relief over being free of him. I had become obsessed with trying to understand the whole affair.

Byron coughed. "Jan…how about another dream?"

"There's only one more."

I'm traveling in Europe with friends, and we go to the opera. I think it's Carmen. *We walk through narrow cobblestone streets to the theater and I'm excited about*

3

seeing the performance. Suddenly it's over and we're coming out of the theater, and I realize I've slept through the whole thing. I'm annoyed at myself, disappointed that I missed the opera.

Byron smirked, "What's *Carmen*?"

"Spanish, a tragedy…"

"I know, I know! It's your life with men and a tragedy. Frankly, you were sleepwalking in your early years. This is your inner life. All the unawareness you lived through. What is *Carmen*? I've seen it numerous times! It's a fucking soap opera. Isn't that what our lives were? Can't we all look back and ask, 'Was that me? Who was leading that life?' We were asleep."

After years of interpreting dreams and past lives together, Byron and I had developed a fast repartee, softened by his humor and sense of irony. Byron was a Jungian analyst and psychic healer, who did a lot of work with dreams, as he considered them a direct connection to the unconscious.

Therapy can be tedious, depressing, and traumatic, but by the time I met Byron I had seen two psychologists and had been through the worst of it. The dream therapy seemed lighter and more revealing than anything I had experienced before.

"What about all the other men?" Byron asked. "And we really need to look at what led up to this. Your mother…"

I cut him off, saying, "I don't want to talk about her. You know I never got along with her. Besides, we've gone over and over it!"

"We still have to look at your anger and try to understand the significance of it."

He really knew how to get to me – bringing up my mother again. I muttered, annoyed, "She was superficial, like her friends in New York. They were always disturbing to me. You know how distant the whole family was. I can't think what else to say about her."

I was particularly devastated now, because I'd recently discovered that I knew only a superficial side of Neil. Byron constantly pointed out a pattern in my relationships with creative men. They were often self-centered and destructive with a dark side that I found mysterious, intriguing, and impenetrable. Even now at age fifty-four, I still agonized over trying to resolve this problem of falling for distant men. Neil, more so than the others, had seemed oddly familiar, which was probably why I felt so comfortable with him. And he was a musician – like my mother.

5

I must have looked disenchanted. Byron said, "OK, let's face it. You're a Green Monkey."

I glared at him and asked, "What's a Green Monkey?"

He smiled. "A Green Monkey is different – he doesn't fit the norm, he's an individual with his own ideas and quirks… You can't do anything about it, so accept it."

"OK. What makes me a Green Monkey?"

He laughed, then explained, "There was a psychological study about the interaction of monkeys. They paint one green to see what happens. He no longer fits in, but he keeps trying because he doesn't know he's green. Everyone else can see how different he is, but he's the last to find out."

I felt worse. "So I have to go on being a Green Monkey for the rest of my life?" I asked.

Byron gave me a sly look. "It's not all that bad," he said. "There are positive aspects to being different. Hell, I'm a Green Monkey, too – probably all artists are." He sighed in deep thought, as though it was inevitable, and then went on. "When you were a kid, you wanted to explore the world without being told how you were supposed to see it and react to it. You lived according to your own terms, hanging on to the joy of living and learning for the sheer love of it. But more important, you were acutely sensitive and learned to refine this sensitivity."

"Yeah, I guess that's true. No one in my family told me how I should see anything! I had no choice – I had to find my own way of seeing things."

"But you were rebelling against the conventional."

"I don't think I was aware of that. You're saying I'm different and that makes my life more difficult."

"Not really. Don't you find friends and family coming to you when they need advice – when they want honest information and need someone they can trust? That's because you worked it all out for yourself and you're not going to give them pat answers. But they also know you care about them."

I began to understand what he was getting at. So the Green Monkey in me had found something intriguing in Neil and needed to find out more about him. Then maybe my curiosity fascinated Neil and drew him to me. I asked Byron, "Does the Green Monkey have a purpose I'm not seeing yet?"

He smiled and said, "In a sense. As you contemplate the Green Monkey, you'll start to understand the theory, but it's something you need to explore on your own."

7

Now I wanted to know more. Byron had perked my interest, inspiring a desire to investigate. "Maybe it would help if I read more about the Green Monkey study," I suggested.

Byron expected my reaction. He said his ex-wife had it and he'd get it for me.

* * *

While driving home I thought about my eccentric mother. She was an outsider in our small town and *different* – certainly a Green Monkey. My mother was Welsh and dramatic and flamboyant; she had also been a nightclub singer. She insisted that I learn music at an early age, believing that a classical background like her own was important for a child. She decided on cello, a large, awkward instrument, as opposed to violin or flute, which I would have preferred.

I guess I was a bit different, too. You weren't supposed to like studying, yet I did. You were expected to like sports and games, but I was lousy at both. I hadn't a clue how to fit in, and having an eccentric, foreign mother didn't help. As a result, I eventually withdrew into my music. I didn't care about relating to kids after a while; I preferred to observe them.

Often I would try to figure out why Mom and I couldn't talk to each other, why she didn't seem to like me, why I disappointed her. And I tried so hard, studying the goddamned cello – trying to please her!

I remembered how my father and I had both withdrawn from Mom at times. She could be intimidating. My father was a sweet, uncomplicated man who adored her. He seemed to idolize her, as she had come from a sophisticated world he had never experienced. He considered her infallible and never questioned her opinions. Unfortunately, as I grew older he began to see me through her eyes. When she said I was difficult, my father believed her.

As a child I wanted to be like my father. I loved doing things with him, especially sledding. Once, when he brought me home with a bloody nose from sledding, my mother yelled at us both. She accused me of loving my father more than her even though he didn't take good care of me. I knew I had to be careful. Even at an early age I sensed her jealousy.

Although at home my mother was either distant or furious, in public she seemed to be a warm and caring person – very much like Neil. The warmth and nurturing that she expressed toward others was what I wanted from her. Because it wasn't given to me, I began to feel

9

abandoned. Now, having lost Neil, I felt helpless and vulnerable as I had when I was that abandoned child.

Not until years later, when I went off to art school in New York, did I begin to feel I belonged. The Abstract Expressionists were in their prime and the art scene was innovative and exciting. Maybe we were all a bunch of Green Monkeys, I thought, rounding a corner to my adobe home.

"But who am I now?" I wondered aloud. My appearance is probably misleading since my Sun is in Pisces, making me an interior, quiet person – the opposite of my mother. But my rising sign, which defines outward expression, is aggressive, positive Aries. Because of this bold exterior, it's hard for even me to see myself clearly!

I never thought I looked very unusual. As a kid, I was tall, thin, gawky, and shy. As I grew older my intense blue eyes and high cheekbones were appealing, but I had no unique traits, nothing that would make anyone stare and say, "Now there's an interesting-looking woman!" In art school my appearance was so conventional that most people thought I would probably drop out. Even my name has no poetry or drama to it – simply Janis Stone. Compared with my mother's name, Lydia Carolina, it sounded dull and flat.

My hair has always been an annoying trait. It's fine and hard to control. I tried blonde streaks and permanents, cutting it, brushing it, and letting it grow, but nothing helped. My hair seems to have an unruly life of its own and I often look disheveled. One day I realized that "being" inside of me has a life of its own, too, which I've tried to ignore although I couldn't ever really get away with it. I've come to realize, through quite a bit of therapy, that's the very "self" I've been trying to find all these years, and I decided it was worth trusting.

CHAPTER TWO

As I walked into the house, it suddenly occurred to me that it was getting late. My best friend, Nina, had invited me to the symphony, the last concert of the winter season. There was to be a large cocktail party before the concert and a reception later for the orchestra members. I would have to dress quickly.

After four years with Neil, I found it difficult going to parties alone and I secretly dreaded the evening, but Nina had insisted. I knew she was trying to get me out more, yet I wondered why I had agreed to go. It was too late to back out. I quelled my anxiety by telling myself that a few hours with good company would be better than another night alone in front of the TV.

Nina picked me up just before sunset, and we drove out into the pinon hills beyond Santa Fe to the first party. We parked on a dirt road and walked up a long driveway, treading dangerously on high heels which were seldom worn in Santa Fe. But this was one of those occasions for dressing up in the elegant local style, with concho belts and tons of turquoise jewelry.

Santa Fe parties are usually very festive, exuding an ambiance I love, but tonight I just wanted to be the observer. It had been fun going to parties with Neil, where people invariably knew him from music scores he had composed for film. He was charming and gregarious, and I had felt attractive and vibrant by his side. He would draw me into conversations, putting his arm around me and looking at me with admiration as though I was an important possession. As much as he loved the attention he generated, he also enjoyed sharing it with me. I had felt very much a part of his life in those days. Now all of that had changed. Who was I without him? I had come to rely on Neil so much I couldn't even remember who I was before we met. Had I given up my independence and my individuality to be with him?

The house was packed with people meandering from the hall to the kitchen, through a small dining room, into a two-story living room and back to the hall. I wandered through the maze feeling strangely disconnected. The kitchen was gigantic and seemed incongruous with the rest of the house. Hors d'oeuvres were being served on a center island. Since it was too noisy for conversation, people just smiled at one another, which was fine with me. I wasn't in a festive mood. Seeing no one I wanted to talk to anyway, I nibbled at shrimp and fattening pastries and moved on.

There was a pianist playing jazz on the upper level of the living room. His style was all too familiar. To avoid pangs of loneliness, I focused instead on the architecture of the room, which was dramatic but not comfortable. The entire house had been remodeled and lacked the charm of most old Santa Fe haciendas with vigas and rough adobe walls, nichos containing santos or Indian kachinas, and a certain warmth that was inherent in the oldness.

I could see Nina across the room deep in conversation with a violinist. Feeling adrift, I cheered up when she came over to me and said, "Why don't we leave and get to the theater before the crowd."

We found our coats and stumbled down the dirt road in the dark to her car. A crowd had already gathered by the time we arrived at the Lensic Theater, a remnant of the past with murals of the Old West. My mood improved as I anticipated the concert and felt the excitement of the chattering audience. Then the lights dimmed, the conductor came on stage to loud applause, and he began conducting Dvorak's *Seventh Symphony*. The slow movement has always been a favorite of mine, with its lyrical yet exhilarating melody. Later I happily escaped into Barber's *Adagio for Strings*. I was feeling elated when it suddenly came to an end, all too soon.

As we were coming out of the theater, it started. My vision began to blur and zigzags darted before my eyes. I had experienced visual migraines before, never knowing what brought them on. Then Byron had said it was a psychic message coming in, and to look at it. I tried, but saw only more zigzags.

Was it caused by associations with my mother? Was that it? I felt stifled by anger just thinking of her. Byron was right – I needed to comprehend this anger. Or did the migraine have to do with Neil, who also loved the thrill of performing? This left me in the background. The thought occurred to me that I wasn't uncomfortable there. It was similar to when I withdrew as a child, only wanting to watch the world going on around me and not have to be a part of it. I didn't want to perform or take a role. I could never have gone on to be a musician; I felt nervous enough having to play for my mother's garden parties and her Christmas programs.

The headache intensified, and my vision became blotchy. Was I unconsciously trying to find a way out of an uncomfortable situation? Obviously I couldn't go to another party with the migraine.

My more social, rational side made me feel that I should try to relate to the group of strangers at the reception, but it was losing the battle. I turned to Nina and said, "I'm afraid I better go home. I hate to desert you, but I've got an awful headache."

Visual migraines sometimes came on when I was under stress. They were a form of release; afterward I could feel the tension drain away, leaving me very relaxed. The psychic aspect was something I had explored, and often when I found the meaning, the headache would clear up. The message could be as simple as, "You don't want to be with this man you're dating." If I couldn't find the message, flashes of neon zigzags and tunnel vision would go on for about a half hour, interfering with my vision and causing me to feel remote and dizzy.

After Nina dropped me off at home, I lay down and let my mind wander. What came to me had nothing to do with either my mother or Neil. Instead, I was seeing colors and shapes. It was time to get to work, to start painting again, to be me.

* * *

The next morning, I stretched a canvas and sat staring at it for a while. Then I started sketching on it in charcoal and was soon involved in the drawing. I worked energetically, feeling the freedom of having time to myself and no deadlines. I could forget everything else in the universe. I would become absorbed in the details of a painting, mixing subtle shades and using transparencies to blend the paint, finding exciting new shapes in forms that were emerging from the charcoal drawings underneath.

But there were other times when I didn't like myself or anything I painted. All I could think of at those moments was that I had been betrayed by a creative, talented man who felt I had no worth. Although a part of me knew it was ridiculous to give him such power over me, depression would take over. I couldn't work and could barely function.

I thought of all the ups and downs and numerous emotions I had experienced that year.

CHAPTER THREE

The next morning as I scrambled eggs, my mind drifted back to thoughts of that last week with Neil. I recalled a dream I had a few days before he left:

I'm in the gym using a treadmill covered with eggshells. There are heavy weights on my shoulders, and I'm feeling terribly stressed.

It didn't take a lot of insight to interpret that one. The tension between us had become intense as Neil gradually drifted away from me.

I remembered how I had felt a sense of freedom and release following his departure. I was at peace in my studio experimenting with soft colors, not wanting to work on anything bright or bold at that time. My soul needed something quiet and sensitive.

While painting, I would put on a tape of pianist Doug Montgomery playing Chopin, never tiring of it, listening to it over and over. It reminded me of Vanessie's, a piano bar in downtown Santa Fe where Doug played. Years ago I would go there late at night to hear him. After the tourists had gone for the winter he didn't need to entertain with show tunes, so he played a lot of Chopin and other classical music – but I particularly remembered the Chopin. There was a familiarity about his music. I had played Chopin as a child, but it was more than that; I felt a deep, unexplainable connection to him.

Sitting on a wide, comfortable sofa, I would sip brandy. It was a cold, snowy winter and there were large fireplaces at each end of the room, with animal skulls above them. In spite of the high-beamed ceiling and vast space, it felt cozy and warm there.

While sitting down to breakfast, I remembered a vivid dream I had soon after Neil left. Set in the nineteenth century, during the time of George Sand and Chopin, I felt sure it revealed a past lifetime I had with Neil:

We lived in a beautiful French country estate, lavishly furnished with floral-patterned draperies and chintz upholstery. We entertained artists and musicians, and I had no real responsibilities. From the bedroom window I could

19

see horse-drawn carriages bringing guests up a long, tree-lined drive. Neil came into the room and asked me to sign some papers. I put my signature on the pages without questioning what they were. I didn't have to, because Neil took care of everything. We were very happy together and I trusted him totally.

Now it occurred to me that our love in that lifetime explained why I trusted him in this lifetime, despite some intuitive sense of his deception.

When I described this dream to Byron, he nodded in recognition of my past-life experience with Neil. He said it was too bad we hadn't known each other about fifteen years ago, when he had the reincarnated George Sand as a patient! I stared at him with a look of skepticism, but he only remarked casually, "It would have been fun to explore that lifetime with her and see what we could remember of the period."

* * *

I spent much of that week reviewing my ten years of therapy with Byron. When I first started, he suggested I read the works of Carl Jung, the Swiss psychotherapist who did extensive work interpreting patients' dreams in the first half of the twentieth century. I delved into the works of Jung and was amazed to discover how much of it extended into realms of synchronicity, parapsychology, and reincarnation.

I had questioned reincarnation after the George Sand dream. Rereading Jung, I saw that he had questioned it, too. Jung noted that the unconscious provides us with more information than the conscious mind and that dreams and other revelations from the unconscious give us good reason to believe in life after death. He wrote that the idea of rebirth is inseparable from that of karma, and if it occurs on a personal level, then we enter life with a preordained destiny based on achievements that took place in our previous lives. Jung's insights validated what I was experiencing in my therapy with Byron, making the esoteric much more credible.

* * *

My earliest dreams while in therapy with Byron were enormously revealing. I would wake up each morning, grab a pen, and jot down all the details I could recall.

Many of my recurrent dreams were about skiing – sometimes when things were going well I'd be sailing downhill. At other times I would find the snow had disappeared halfway down the mountain, or I would suddenly lose my poles, making it difficult to traverse through my life.

There were also dreams of hotels and houses – going from one to another, never feeling secure or settled. Byron said the houses had to do with figuring out my structure, getting it in order, and straightening out the emotional chaos of this lifetime. Although some houses were familiar, others were strictly creations of my unconscious – extraordinary spaces I had never seen before, inhabited by strangers with odd-looking faces. One was a gay man, tall and thin with long blond hair, wearing a wide-brimmed lavender hat:

I meet the blond man and tell him I know he is living in my house in Los Angeles. He sheepishly pulls the hat down over his eyes.

Was this a disguise for my male side that I was perhaps ignoring?

Soon afterward, Byron and I explored Jung's theory of the anima, the repressed feminine in the male psyche, and the animus, the repressed masculine in the female psyche both of which powerfully influence our behavior. Byron explained, "We project the anima or animus onto the opposite sex, which often accounts for the experience of falling in love with someone we hardly know, who is actually someone who fulfills the hidden qualities we seek, consciously or unconsciously."

I smiled and said, "So that's why we can fall in love with someone across a room."

He nodded in agreement. "But often this ideal contains a shadow animus which is why the same dark, destructive types can keep appearing in our lives. The presence of a shadow animus could explain some of *your* relationships."

This was certainly true, I thought to myself. Before I met Neil I was seeing Byron, trying to comprehend my relationships with creative types who were irresponsible and sometimes alcoholic, but I had not recognized how destructive they could be. One was Gregory, a free spirit high on life. Maybe it was the expansiveness of the drugs or alcohol, but there was something magical about Gregory, even though he eventually drank himself off the planet. That was when I started seeing Byron, which was fortunate since my father, Gregory, and Heathcliff, my Russian Blue, all died within two months of one another, leaving me feeling miserable, lonely, and deserted.

I remember asking Byron why I continued to get involved with dark shadow types. He had looked at me with an intense stare and explained, "That's what we have to work on. We continue to repeat the same pattern until we learn how to transform the old animus developed in childhood into a functional one. But first we need to learn

23

what is hidden in the shadow. That's where much of the true self resides. When we see this, we are no longer willing to be as unconscious.

It sounded plausible at the time, but I wasn't at all sure how this transformation occurred, or if I could change my animus and thus my self.

In fact, after the trauma of my affair with Neil and all the work I had done with Byron, it appeared I still had not succeeded in transforming my animus into a functional, positive one. I began to wonder: could therapy *really* change my life?

CHAPTER FOUR

For days I dwelled on thoughts of Gregory and of my first year in Santa Fe. Gregory not only exuded charm but seemed to live in a state of euphoria, and I felt elated in his presence. Although I could tell he had a brilliant mind, I was surprised to learn he had once been a data processor creating computer programs – in his more sober days, I assumed.

Friends in California had told me to call Gregory when I first came to visit Santa Fe. We hit if off immediately. Soon after my move from Los Angeles the following year, Gregory invited me to a party where I met artists, psychics, astrologers, and many other people who were involved in metaphysics and spirituality. I expected to find a rather woo-woo crowd with hippie overtones, and was surprised to

25

meet quite conventional-looking people who took their inquiries into the esoteric very seriously. Some women were dressed in colorful, ethnic dresses; most of the men wore boots, and western shirts with scarves. All were quite attractive.

Among the many intriguing people I met was a stylish, gray-haired British woman, and I wondered what could be her connection to these people. Later I learned she channeled a spirit guide from the world beyond and she was referred to as the English Channel!

From the kitchen I could see Gregory in the living room entertaining people with a new poem, his long arms flailing and his eyes flashing. He was reciting, "In the middle of day, or dark of night, it's all about de-light..." Dear Gregory – expressive, flattering, flamboyant, as I now realized, much like my mother! But his warmth and enthusiasm, unlike hers, made me feel alive. I wondered now if he was manic-depressive. When he was up he was magic, but when he was down he was drunk.

I even tried LSD with him, jumping from one fantasy to another. At one point I was hanging on to a large falcon, about to fly with it but suddenly deciding to let it go, much preferring to stay on earth. Besides, I was afraid of heights. Years later, to my amazement, Neil moved in with a sculpture that was a replica of the Maltese Falcon – the very bird I had been hanging on to!

I had consulted astrologers and numerologists previously, finding their readings to be amazingly accurate, and I knew I was often led by intuition. But never before had I understood the many facets of spirituality or how it could guide my life. With Gregory I began to comprehend so much more and started to trust my own psychic abilities.

Gregory introduced me to Byron at that party. He took my hand and said, "I want you to meet an unusual therapist," while leading me over to a quiet, serious man with thick glasses. I was somewhat intimidated, for he seemed to look right through me. But I soon learned this was only an act he put on to avoid partaking in small talk, and lurking underneath was a vibrant, humorous man. A few years later, when I began therapy with him, I had no idea what sort of change this creative trip through the mind would eventually bring.

For many years after embarking on therapy, feeling upset and not knowing why, I dashed off to see Byron, only to have him point out the effect of my karma from past lives and lessons I needed to learn from it. One of my earliest dreams, soon after that party, seemed to be about the English Channel:

27

I attend a concert. There's a gray-haired woman sitting next to me. She's attractive and dignified. She says she's really looking forward to the concert as works by this composer are seldom played. But there's a delay and the audience is asked to step outside. When we file back in, most of the people don't return to their seats but instead turn around and continue right up the same aisle to the exit. I don't see the woman and I wonder when the concert will begin.

I stop for dinner on the way home. A woman is cooking lamb in laurel leaves. She says she gets the leaves and firewood from Steve. She tells me Steve took my dinner home to me. Then I see a giant turtle and start chopping at its shell with an ax. I'm trying to kill it!

After listening intently to the dream, Byron said, "I think she's a counterpart developing in you. This is a wise woman archetype, representing individuality."

I replied, "Yes, she seems very strong and doesn't fit into the crowd at the concert."

Byron grimaced, adding, "And the concert never begins. You're not ready to have this experience yet – the concert of life. The woman has everything intact and radiates character, the real thing." He leaned back and continued, "So, you're going to be fed the sacrificial lamb cooked in laurel leaves. What's laurel?"

"A tree ..."

Byron, in his enthusiasm, cut in, "A very potent plant representing victory as in 'crown of laurels'! And Steve, a male, provides the heat and the laurel, the alchemy for cooking."

"But he runs off with my dinner!"

Byron retorted, "All the men have run off with your dinner. Who the fuck stayed around to nourish you in a loving and intimate way? So, who's Steve?"

I thought about this question for a moment before answering, "He's a young contractor who helps me with repairs. He comes up with creative ideas and he's reliable. I think he's happy in his marriage, so I would say his life seems pretty much together."

Byron said, "He's sounds like a potent animus. Compared with Gregory, he would appear to be a productive, responsible person. But then there's this turtle. Holy shit! A turtle is a big-time symbol, representing ancient wisdom and knowledge."

"I've been given two turtles for good luck – one by an Italian artist, as a token of our long friendship, and one by a former boyfriend while we were breaking up!"

29

Byron nodded, "Very powerful, very wise. So you're hacking away at the turtle, trying to get nourishment from it. In a sense that turtle is power. I think the essence of the dream has to do with your fear of power."

I looked at my notes. "Oh, I almost forgot to mention that I woke up depressed and angry after the dream," I said, not wanting to ignore this issue any longer. "I thought the reason might have something to do with the concert that never began. I never hear the music I expected to find with men, which makes me angry and disappointed."

Byron said, "Yes, I like that interpretation. All anger is ultimately self-anger. It's anger and shame from not being loved in childhood, not feeling loved by the universe. We're not living in enough love. Ultimately everyone wants a nice, warm, intimate working marriage – warmth and intimacy."

I asked, "Why can't we find it?"

"Because of our karma shit. We came into this lifetime to work out debts from past lives. We were given families of origin to allow us to understand what love is. You can have love when you're no longer needy and co-dependent!" He paused for a moment, deep in thought, then said, "Now, back to the turtle. The hacking of the turtle might represent your anger at this unfulfilled archetype."

"That makes more sense."

"You're frustrated and angry about not having enough love, so you're lashing out at the turtle, still trying to get at it in a primitive way. Now, how do we get at it in a non-primitive way?"

"You're asking *me*?"

Byron smiled. "I'm gonna tell you. You get on its back and ride it, then it takes you somewhere. We're closer in this dream. It's a killer, isn't it? I talk a lot, but we'll get there eventually, kiddo."

*   *   *

I remember seeing for the first time how my dreams expressed my feelings and anger. I was stunned to realize I had never expressed feelings of anger anywhere but in my dreams. Something had obviously blocked any awareness of my emotions.

Now, many years later, looking back at that dream, I recalled how distant and unloved I had felt as a child. I decided to ride the turtle of wisdom and self-knowledge to see where it would take me. I knew the answers were in my past, and it was necessary to relive some of those painful and lonely experiences in order to understand the person I had become.

PART II

Neil

CHAPTER FIVE

The following week I spent a lot of time gardening and thinking. As I dug up weeds and planted flowers, my mind wandered back to my life in Los Angeles. I had moved there after ten difficult years in New York.

From the start, what I liked most about Los Angeles was that you could live in the hills, and feel like you were secluded in the country and still be in the middle of the city. I had a little Spanish house nestled under large pines and eucalyptus trees. It was there, hidden among all the new condominiums in the Hollywood Hills, that I had first met Neil, nearly six years ago.

The house was set way back from the street, and my garden attracted the neighborhood cats, as it was a jungle of yuccas, agaves, geraniums and six-foot-high jade. I knew

35

nothing about gardening then and the only plants that survived were those that didn't need much help. The garden also had bougainvilla clinging to evergreen trees twenty feet above the house. I had let everything grow and grow in an attempt to block out the impending rash of new buildings.

Years ago when I bought that house on Jacaranda Street, I was told it had been built about 1930 by a Spanish dancer named José. There was a large living room with high sloping beams, and a lovely arch separating it from the dining room which was two steps up, creating a perfect stage for dancers. The story was that José performed there to raise money for starving artists during the Depression, and ever since the house was inhabited by artists. It was small, but to me it was a paradise. My father, finally resigned to the fact that I was never returning home, helped me with the down payment. Life here was easier, and I felt relaxed after the rat race of my years in New York.

I had bought the house when the former owner died. Not wanting to live there alone, his partner had decided to move to France and put the house on the market, leaving behind exquisite antiques and furniture. The library I inherited contained many classics and art books printed prior to the 1940s. Looking through the old books, I often came across letters and postcards from the artist's friends in Italy, many describing the situation in Europe before World War II. They gave a personal aura to the house that made it feel like a home, especially after my small New York apartment.

The garden was delightful with large urns and European plaques on the patio walls. There were also two statues of Saint Francis – one in a fountain by the front door and the other in a shrine by the wrought iron gates leading into the front patio. These personal touches made it a very special place to live. At last I was settled, which gave me a security I had never felt before.

The house also had a ghost who I thought might be José. At first he frightened me. I would wake up to find a light on in the hallway, knowing that it was off when I went to bed and fearing someone was in the house. But I came to realize he was only being playful and wanted me to be aware of his presence. One of his favorite pranks was tampering with the locks. There were French doors opening to a small patio out back, with stairs leading up to a guest room over the garage. When I moved to Santa Fe twelve years later, I decided to rent my lovely house rather than sell it, but each time I showed it to prospective renters I couldn't unlock the door to the patio. Then when the people had left, it opened easily.

One day a handyman I knew came by to repair the guest room shower fixtures upstairs. We both tried to open the French doors to the patio, but they wouldn't budge. Finally I announced, "It's only a friend to do repairs. He doesn't want to rent the house." Immediately the key turned and the door opened. Probably the ghost didn't want a new occupant around who might give him a hard time. We were pals by now.

*   *   *

I had been renting the house to a cocaine dealer for the past year. Of course, I wasn't aware of Ramon's occupation when I agreed to rent to him. The real estate broker said he was very nice and paid in cash, so I went along with his judgment rather than my own intuition. I had a feeling I should meet him, but I had already moved to Santa Fe and didn't want to make the trip to Los Angeles. In fact, I never did meet Ramon. But the neighbors all knew him and would call me with reports of police busts, a Rolls Royce and other traffic in and out, gunshots and more. But the rental laws in the area were all in his favor and there was no way I could evict him. I was helpless and could do nothing about their complaints.

Ramon had lived there for about a year when I heard that he had been arrested and sent to jail. Greatly relieved, I flew back to Los Angeles to make repairs and search for a new tenant. I was shocked to find he left a few young prostitutes in my house, who left their stiletto heel marks in the oak floors, but they were so sweet that I couldn't complain of the damage. Instead, I began to worry where they would go.

A few days later I put a rental ad in the paper, and Neil showed up to see the house. I liked him immediately – an older, stable man, a successful musician who had led what sounded like an idyllic existence with his wife and daughter in Oregon, but who was now divorced and trying to put his life back together. (I probably had some similar fantasy about Ramon to have rented it to him the previous year, but I don't quite remember.)

However, Neil didn't rent my house, which disappointed me. It was too small and not secluded enough for him. He liked to compose late into the night and was afraid of disturbing the neighbors with his music.

But the next day, as I was working in my crummiest jeans, he came up the driveway. This time I observed him closely. He was tall and thin, with a straight nose, a sensual mouth and a happy expression on his face. He had whiffs of graying hair that stuck out at the sides, giving him a casual, humorous look. Not terribly handsome, I told myself, but all in all he had a comfortable presence that I liked.

After we talked for a while, he said he would like to see me again, and asked me to call him the next time I was in Los Angeles, so he could take me out to dinner.

For days I thought about him. He didn't seem to fit my usual pattern of attractive but noncommittal, interesting but impractical, amusing but unstable – I could go on and on about the men who had populated my life over the past few years. He was nice-looking in a mature way, and intelligent... That was it! He seemed real, solid, right there. In the past, I had been attracted to men who were good-looking but egotistical. In contrast, he appeared to be stable – *that* was what I liked. I sensed I could probably develop a strong relationship with this kind of man.

It was a year later when I returned to Los Angeles and I had put Neil out of my mind. Then on a whim, I called him and he said he knew of a great restaurant where he'd like to take me.

He walked up the driveway wearing a bright shirt and a floppy hat. I wondered if I looked too formal in my light mauve dress and sandal strap heels, but these thoughts evaporated as we drove off and he pulled up to one of my favorite Indian restaurants. The smell of cumin and coriander greeted us the moment the door opened. Neil ordered specialties I had never tasted and we proceeded to gorge on delicious exotic dishes flavored with spicy herbs. The Indian music further enhanced the magic in the air that night.

Partway through dinner, Neil leaned across the table and took my hand, saying, "It's good being together, isn't it?"

Flattered, I smiled and answered, "It is. I was thinking the same thing!" We both laughed.

The evening was very romantic until Neil started talking about the *Course in Miracles*, which he was studying. I was bored but couldn't figure out how to change the subject. Besides, he seemed unstoppable. The more he went on and on about miracles, the more my spirits gradually descended. I didn't believe in miracles.

It's not that I don't like the idea of miracles, but I have a very practical side that is suspect of depending on them. I think I prefer the concept of angels out there guiding us, rather than rescuing us. I've known people who look for miracles, particularly when they need money. They are sure it will come to them, if they concentrate on the need and

41

have faith in the principle. I've never seen this approach actually work.

To me a miracle is something unexpected and delightful that just happens, or something astounding with no explanation, so I've always refused to rely on miracles to solve my problems.

But the following year a miracle occurred. I received a call from Neil on July first. Out of the blue, "Hey, I'm on my way to Santa Fe, and wanted to make sure you were there," he said.

Shocked, I blurted out, "That's wonderful!" Since I hadn't heard from him for so long, I had given up any subliminal hopes that our brief encounters could develop into a relationship. But he asked if he could stay with me and I heartily said yes.

I was thrilled at the prospect of his visit. I realized that despite our differing views of angels, I had been very attracted to him and was terribly excited about seeing him again. And I had been trying to tell myself he meant nothing to me! Fate, I told myself, was right there from the start!

CHAPTER SIX

When we discussed that first visit with Neil, Byron had questions about my impressions of him – how I felt with Neil and how close we were. As I reflected, it all seemed too good to be true at that time.

Neil arrived in Santa Fe with his friend, Sam, the day before the Fourth of July. Despite the year that had passed since our dinner together, we felt an immediate rapport. Obviously we had known each other in a previous lifetime to feel so comfortable together.

He hugged me and exclaimed, "Janis, let me look at you. It's been much too long." I beamed.

I remembered that same warm smile and felt like melting. Still, I decided to put him in the guest room, telling myself, "Be cautious this time. You've made a lot of mistakes by jumping in too fast."

Early that evening Sam went off with friends, and Neil and I had dinner out on the deck. I lit candles creating a romantic setting against the dim lights of the garden. We talked and laughed about everything – that is, except our personal lives, which we touched on minimally. He, especially, seemed hesitant about discussing his former wife and daughter. Nevertheless, he was bright and articulate and the evening was everything I had anticipated.

On the Fourth of July, we went to the Plaza for the annual pancake breakfast. A band was playing and there were long lines for the pancakes. The whole town came out for the event! We sat on the grass eating heavy pancakes covered with a thin slice of ham. Neil commented in his charming way, "You know, we've both spent so many years in cities, but isn't this much more fun?"

I agreed and said to Sam, "It makes you feel like you're in a small town, doesn't it?"

He looked at me in his droll way, replying, "Ahh, you *are* in a small town." I guess I had never thought of Santa Fe as a town, but he was right. It was small, even though it seemed like a city as it had so many cultural events and interesting galleries.

Sam was visiting old friends in Santa Fe, but he spent a lot of time with us. As he and Neil had known each other for years, the dialogue between them was fast and humorous. I enjoyed Sam's sense of humor, and there was a twinkle in his eyes over a rambling nose and a small mouth that got screwed up in an expressive way when he talked. His graying hair was at an unfortunate length, probably on its way to being a ponytail, giving him a maiden aunt look.

Later that day, the three of us went to the Indian dances at Nambe Pueblo where we climbed up to a waterfall high in the hills. Neil and I kept staring at each other. Was this really happening? I felt like a happy visitor myself going to all the tourist attractions with them. After the dances, we drove out to Bandelier National Monument and walked back to the ruins left by ancient cliff dwellers. Neil and Sam climbed high up into the caves and waved to me. As I smiled back, I felt a warmth inside that had been missing from my life. While they explored the kivas, I made friends with some deer that were obviously used to people coming into their territory. Then I sat on a large rock thinking what a lovely day it had been. I couldn't remember when I'd had company I enjoyed so much.

At home that night, Neil and I curled up on the couch in my studio and listened to tapes of his compositions. I discovered I liked his music. It was melodic yet it contained surprising passages similar to Poulenc's. Bursts of emotion erupted out of ordered, rational themes.

The next day Neil met some of my friends, who were charmed by his wit and flattered by his attention. I was very happy with this dynamic man!

That night we sat in the studio talking, with Paul Simon's *Graceland* playing in the background – light and soaring music that made everything feel mellow and right with the world: "Diamonds on the souls of our shoes." Everyone reaches heights in their lives and this seemed to be one of those ascending times of creativity and love, of new rhythms and sounds:

"These are the days of miracles and wonder.
We look to a distant constellation that's lying in a corner of the sky!"

On the third night of Neil's visit, I smiled at him and said, "You know, more than anything, I think I just want to hold you all night and be close." He spent that night with me and it was everything I could have dreamed – lazy, sensual and warm. And I thought I had found it all.

* * *

Neil extended his trip for another week so we could get to know each other better. There was so much we wanted to do together. I had never been to a rodeo, and he insisted on taking me after we got stuck in a traffic jam while the rodeo parade passed by.

Another evening we attended the Santa Fe Chamber Music Festival in the old St. Francis Auditorium, known for its murals of the life of St. Francis on the walls and high, painted beams with carved corbels on the ceiling. It felt like a chapel but was actually part of the Fine Arts Museum and had been built for concerts. The chamber music was always a treat with excellent musicians from all over the world. That was a big draw and had a lot to do with his decision to make the move.

During that week Neil had intended to spend a few hours each day looking at houses, with the thought of moving to Santa Fe. It would be an easy commute to Los Angeles for business, he figured, and he'd much prefer to live and write music in this peaceful setting. But our days were filled with sightseeing and adventures, leaving little time for house hunting.

Then one morning at breakfast he asked, "How would you feel about me moving in with you for a while?"

Stifling my excitement, I tried to sound practical, answering, "Might be a good idea. We'd have to work out studio space and a few things."

He quickly said, "It wouldn't be a problem. We could find another studio, I'm sure. But would you really like to be together?"

"Of course I would. I was dreading the thought of you leaving."

"So was I," he confessed, wrapping his arms around me and holding me tight. Then we discussed more details, hesitantly at first, and finally decided we could be very happy living together – at least until Neil found a house.

It was a few months before he made the big move. In the meantime, we made numerous trips back and forth between Santa Fe and Los Angeles, so anxious to see each other. Then he finally managed to sublet his home there and suddenly we were together!

*   *   *

Now all that seems so long ago! I didn't have any doubts at the time and we *were* close!

CHAPTER SEVEN

I smiled to myself as I remembered that first year. Siegfried arrived with Neil that January, when he first came to live in Santa Fe. I knew he was bringing Siegfried and had my reservations, but there was no alternative — I had to introduce him to my cats, Bootsie and Sage. Bootsie, who wore a black mask and a tuxedo coat over his white chest and boots, stared in disbelief. Sage, in her elegant way, sat with her feet together and tail wrapped around them looking curiously at Siegfried from a high banco. I thought they would, in time, adjust.

Siegfried was a big grey cat and very lovable, not like my eccentric alley cats who still shied away from people. They were polite and hid from Siegfried at first. Gradually they began to accept him, but Siegfried took over, in a sense

49

like Neil, as he was obviously more aggressive and the dominant cat. It was never totally resolved.

I was at that first stage of an affair, the excitement of the attraction – that inner undeniable happiness, the glow I felt that seemed to radiate everywhere. Getting to know each other became an adventure. An astrologer had said my Venus was in Aquarius and that meant an attraction had to be mental as well as physical for me, and Neil seemed to have all the right qualities.

The first year together was romantic and fun. We never got around to looking for a house for Neil. In fact, neither of us ever brought it up. I loved coming home in the evening and cooking dinner for the two of us. I loved having his arms around me all night – I was in love, and I think he felt the same. The loneliness had gone out of my life.

That summer we would go down to the Farmers' Market on Saturday mornings for fresh corn, tomatoes just picked from the garden and all sorts of homemade breads and jellies. In his gregarious way, Neil would stop and talk to the farmers about the weather and crops. He really seemed to feel a part of the small town.

The market was very crowded one Saturday when I noticed a woman waving and fighting the crowd coming toward us. I couldn't place her and then, suddenly, Neil's arms were around her and he was kissing her. He let her go and introduced us: "This is Kali," he beamed. Turning to her he said, "And this is Jan who I mentioned to you." It sounded like an afterthought. She looked a bit blank.

I guess I was obviously cool so he broke it off and we wandered on. I glared at him, "Who was that?"

"Oh, just someone I met having coffee one morning. She's a guitarist." And he dismissed it.

I was jealous, but I didn't want him to know. I couldn't get used to his friendliness with women. They all seemed to like him and obviously he loved women.

*   *   *

As it turned out, Neil worked at home and I decided to rent a nearby studio that summer. I wanted to do some larger paintings to experiment with new ideas, so I liked having a separate space. Each morning I would ride my bicycle about a mile up Canyon Road to the studios that had once been the New School. They were situated in a low area along the Santa Fe River surrounded by trees and it felt good to paint there away from all interruptions. My studio was one big room with nothing in it. I furnished it with only an easel, a table, paints, brushes and a CD player.

Fredericka Heller

As I was stretching a canvas one morning, a dream kept coming back to me – bit by bit until the whole thing began to make sense. When I got home, I called Byron and made an appointment.

Byron felt very positive about my relationship with Neil at that time and my dreams reflected all sorts of progress. In fact, Neil was having therapy sessions with Byron, too, and liked him immensely.

I went in to see Byron the next morning still excited about the dream. He greeted me at the door and led me into his office. "I haven't seen you for awhile, Jan. I want to hear what's going on with you and Neil. And what's this dream?"

I beamed, "It's about my work, only I'm a sculptor in this one. I can see it's very positive but I wanted to get your interpretation." I paused, before going on with the dream.

I'm in the country at the home of Howard and Elsa, two art dealers from New York. Everyone is excited about my new work. I've put together blocks of wood for models of the new sculptures. They offer me a show in New York and ask me to drive Howard to his apartment in the city. I start off in Elsa's little Fiat and have trouble backing out of the driveway. I'm nervous not knowing what to talk about with Howard. Although I don't know where the apartment is,

somehow we finally get there. He wants me to show with a
sculptor who works with sound so we go to see his work.

Byron smiled, "Sounds like the building blocks of a
new life. This is a success dream. At last you're capturing
some of the authority you never felt in New York – coming
more into the self."

"And I think this in some way has to do with Neil – a
sculptor who works with sound. Maybe he has a role in
sculpting my life at this point."

Byron nodded in agreement, "Yes, yes…"

"There are a few things I don't get. What about the
little Fiat? Why can't I back it out of the driveway?

"Have you ever owned a Fiat?"

"I did once in California. It wasn't a very good car."

Byron frowned, "I had one. It was a disaster, always
being repaired."

"So was mine!"

He laughed, "It's an ominous warning sign, unreliable,
implying peril. But on another level, you're just having
difficulty getting the success vehicle moving – coming into
the self. But you're driving the woman's car. She was a
well-known dealer, right?"

"Yes, Elsa was one of the most respected women in the
art world."

Fredericka Heller

"Come on. You're dealing with the heavy hitters here and it's scary. Look, you grew up in a very patriarchal world. Men got all the credit in that era. Women worked behind the scenes and accepted it. But you're building new models!"

I added, "Women weren't supposed to be successful – it wasn't feminine or something?? Unless there was a famous man behind a woman artist, saying 'look at this artist', there wasn't much chance of getting exhibited. It didn't do any good to be aggressive."

Byron said, "Right. You were programed not to succeed creatively, but all that's changed. And psychologically you've grown to the point that you can accept success now."

* * *

I went home feeling as though I was starting a new life. It was exciting. I walked into the house and into Neil's arms.

He smiled and said he had a surprise for me, "I've been looking at trucks. You're going to need one to move those big paintings so I've put a deposit on a little red Toyota. Do you want to go to see it?"

Thinking of how considerate he was and picking up on his enthusiasm, I said, "Of course."

54

But on the way to the dealer I did think of how expensive this would be and we didn't really need a truck. He was working on a big commission, but I knew it wasn't finished. I had no idea when he would get a check for it. He never wanted to discuss finances and I was the one who took care of most of the bills. Then I got annoyed at myself for being so practical. I didn't want to put a damper on his enthusiasm, so I kept my mouth shut. I had to trust him.

We bought the truck and it was fun owning something together. I would see him driving around town in the red truck, looking very much a part of Santa Fe. After all, every macho man in town drove a truck!

I was happy with our life. There was so much we enjoyed together. Towards the end of summer a big benefit was held to raise money for the Santa Fe Art Institute. This was a unique school that brought master artists to Santa Fe. Anyone could apply to work with them for a month at a time and I had taken two classes with painters from New York. The other artists in the class were advanced, so it was a stimulating experience that influenced my work. I began to simplify shapes, and working with pastels gave me a new perspective on color. There were many dinner parties where we discussed painting well into the night. I hadn't been so immersed in my work since art school.

Now all of the alumni were asked to paint pictures of animals dancing to be auctioned off at a "Barnyard Party." Of course, I painted my cats dancing under the stars in a field of daisies.

Neil laughed when he saw the painting and said, "I'm not sure I want you to sell that one. You've really captured Bootsie and Sage."

The party, which turned out to be great fun, was held in a large riding ring at a nearby ranch. After bidding on some of the more outrageous paintings, I came away with one of a flamboyant chicken. Then it was time for the pig races. Actually they were giant hogs dressed in tutus egged on by food thrown in their path.

Along with a delicious barbeque, we gorged on hot New Mexican dishes with lots of red chile. There was a good country western band, and I even convinced Neil to try dancing with me. Everything was fun that summer!

In the fall, I took Neil to Fiesta, a big Hispanic event held every September. One of the highlights of Fiesta was the burning of Zozobra. I assumed Zozobra was an early pagan Spanish figure, but I learned he was created in the twenties by a Santa Fe artist, Will Schuster, and his friends. They made a huge effigy of an ugly creature they called Old Man Gloom, Zozobra in Spanish. Then they burned him in a big bonfire to get rid of gloom and doom for the year ahead.

As we walked toward the park with the crowd, I told Neil how Zozobra had become a tradition. I rambled on, "He's grown to forty-feet tall and his burning takes place every year at the opening of Fiesta, along with lots of dancers and fireworks that are part of the ceremony."

We stood in the back of the field watching Zozobra burn as thousands of people cheered him on, yelling: "Burn him, burn him!" I recalled what an emotional experience it was the first time, and then it became an event I looked forward to each year.

Neil loved the whole pagan ritual. He was yelling with the crowd. As we walked to the Plaza afterwards, he had his arm around me and said, "This is the beginning of our second year together and what a great way to start it – no gloom and doom!"

PART III

A Falling Apart Year

CHAPTER EIGHT

Now, reflecting on our life together, I tried to see when it first started to fall apart. Time seemed to go fast as we were both busy with our work during the next few years. Neil was often in Los Angeles composing scores, but it didn't bother me as I felt confident in our relationship. In fact I valued the time to be alone as I was working on paintings for an exhibit.

In time, however, the relationship gradually seemed to be disintegrating. I felt a distance growing between us. We started having sessions together with Byron and seemed to be making progress. Yet I found that getting to know Neil was full of mystery. I tried to piece his life together to see the whole person, but there were gaps I couldn't comprehend.

One Halloween Eve I picked Neil up at the airport in Albuquerque when he was coming back from Los Angeles. He gave me one of those distant smiles, as though he was somewhere else, and kissed me absent-mindedly. I wondered what that was about.

Perhaps we were spending too much time apart. I realized I had always been a bit of a loner, enjoying time painting and reading in solitude, but I wondered now if I neglected him too much. I was sure it was my own fault. I wasn't affectionate enough. I was still in my head. Was it too late to change? There was no point in asking him what I had done wrong. He would only deny anything was wrong.

I pushed my thoughts aside and enthusiastically told him we were invited to a dinner party that night, so we needed to rush home if we were going to get there on time. Two well-known jazz musicians would be there and I had Halloween costumes all ready for us. I thought he would be excited about it, but he seemed determined to take his time, even stopping for gas. He didn't say much about his trip and I sensed that something was terribly wrong.

When we finally got home, I dashed around getting the costumes together. I was determined to get to the party and my excitement finally seemed to catch on. We were only an hour late arriving and everyone was in high spirits. But I knew there was something he wasn't telling me and the thought bothered me all night. It was stuck in the back of my mind.

One of the rewards that comes only in time, when your lives seem to mesh, is that feeling of intimacy and closeness which leads to trust. It was a long time before I began to realize we weren't getting there.

CHAPTER NINE

Byron could see it all happening. He asked me to look back at specific incidents. I realized that I became aware of Neil's distance in little ways at first. He would sit and stare at the television for hours. One night, I sat down beside him and he just kept looking straight ahead at the TV. I tried to talk to him, but he seemed distracted and ignored me. I sensed an underlying hostility in Neil I couldn't comprehend. He no longer put his arm around me when I curled up next to him on the couch, and it felt uncomfortable and disturbing.

One morning he was playing solitaire. I knew he did this when he had a block. It was a sort of preoccupation for part of his brain, so that the rest of it could wander freely and creatively in other areas. At first I found this upsetting and thought it was another way of locking me out, but later I came to understand the process as I related it to painting. I usually played loud music when I was at work in my studio. Often I didn't even hear it, but it blocked out certain noises and disturbances so I could concentrate better on the painting. At the same time, the energy of the music propelled me into the painting.

This particular morning, Neil seemed very down when I went into his studio. I looked over his shoulder and said, "There's a move."

This seemed to annoy him, but he didn't say anything.

"Can I be of any help?"

He mumbled, "I'm trying to work out a difficult passage."

I knew music, so I asked, "Can I hear it?"

He didn't look up, "No, I can't play it for you. I don't trust *anyone's* opinion at this point." He sounded angry.

He didn't trust me enough to let me hear it! I really felt rejected this time and at a loss as to how to relate to him. There was an edge of cruelty to all of this. How could he say he didn't trust me? I slammed the door and left.

I began to realize there was a deep, dark side to Neil that I was never going to reach. In my perception, he seemed to be implying, "That's all you're going to know about me. To reveal more could give you ammunition to use against me. I don't trust beyond this point." He had broken off many relationships in the past, and I began to see that he feared to go beyond a certain point – a point that involved openness, trust and intimacy.

*   *   *

I know now it was the shadow side that perhaps Neil couldn't accept in himself. I called Byron to make an appointment as I needed to discuss what was happening.

Byron explained, "Often the qualities we have denied in our life don't go away, but are just relegated to the unconscious, becoming the shadow. We don't want this side to be seen."

I said, "You know, I think I've been fascinated with the shadow most of my life, but I never really understood its meaning in that sense. Do you think it's a perverse quality in me that wanted to stay distant and avoid intimacy?"

Byron answered, "Not necessarily a perverse quality. You grew up in a distant family. You were a private person and that was comfortable for you."

I thought about this as I stared out the window, "You can imagine all sorts of wonderful qualities lurking underneath when men are so mysterious about themselves!"

Byron continued, "Yes, that's true. Then, of course, there's the face we present to the world, our persona. When people are stuck in their persona we see only the facade – they quite literally lack depth and appear shallow to us."

As I drove home from that session I realized I had been blind to an awareness of the shadow during those blissful years with Neil. I had accepted his persona as real, seeing only what I chose to see, only the good side with numerous "rationales" to explain the inconsistencies. I was so sure Neil was right for me and so determined to make the relationship work, that it took me a long time to see all the clues that dropped before me. The realization was scary and I felt at a loss as to what I should do.

I was searching for answers and explanations in Jungian books when I came across the archetype of the Demon Lover, described as the Vampire. He represented the essence of evil's attraction, seductive and possessive. As he uses his power to find victims, others willingly give up their selves to him. It stated that the Demon Lover personifies an addictive and possessive form of imprisonment, easy to slide into.

It occurred to me that Neil had this kind of seductive charm and I could easily become his victim, getting caught up in his charisma and enthusiasm, never realizing how he stole energy from me. Or was I becoming paranoid?

I knew now that Neil had simply given me the image he thought I wanted of him. It was the safest way for him, but he remained an enigma to me and I really didn't know him. Was I dealing with a con artist? The lying wasn't so disturbing – it was what he kept hidden. This was becoming more and more evident as I became healthier and less attracted to the shadow. That kind of mystery no longer appealed to me.

Neil was fine on stage, like my mother, but when it came to intimate communication, he seemed incapable. Maybe we had both withdrawn into our own abstract worlds of music and creativity at an early age, not finding the nurturing we needed in our parents. Probably I was no better than Neil at relating, only I wanted the closeness that seemed to be waning away. I was terribly upset and didn't know what to do about it. Probing the situation and trying to reach him only made matters worse. No doubt this was terribly threatening to a man who was used to denying his feelings.

CHAPTER TEN

At my next appointment with Byron, he seemed intent on getting me away from this heavy reflection. He was in a particularly playful frame of mind.

He asked, almost jokingly, "See if you can think of a relationship that didn't fit this destructive pattern of shadow men who came on to you and then neglected you or let you down. Maybe the reason you haven't found a committed relationship is that you haven't been looking for one."

His comment made me think. Yes, I knew that was partly true. I said, a bit sheepishly, "OK, there was the trip to Turkey when I met Gunsel — romantic, fun, exciting. He was a gorgeous captain in the Turkish navy.

Byron seemed surprised, "How did you meet him?"

"I went on a cruise with my father after my mother died. The captain of the ship invited me to dinner in Istanbul along with some other people on the cruise. We went up the Bosphorus Strait to a small seafood restaurant near the Black Sea. Gunsel, a friend of the captain's, sat next to me."

"And…"

Lost in pleasant memories of feeling in love, I continued, "Gunsel returned to the ship with me, and we danced the evening away. He even met my father and asked for permission to visit me in the States. He seemed so proper. My father found him charming, and encouraged him to visit me. Well, Gunsel came to see me in California the next year, and we went to Mexico for a vacation. I never told my father about that!"

"So it turned into a good relationship?"

"Yes, we had a great time together and he invited me to visit him in Turkey the following year. I think we saw all the mosques in Istanbul, and then we drove down to Bodrum and stopped to see the ruins at Ephesus. It was so foreign, nothing like Europe, and very few people spoke any English."

"Why did the relationship end?"

"After that trip I broke it off. Gunsel wanted marriage, but there were so many cultural differences and I could never have lived in Istanbul. I guess we didn't have the kind of closeness we needed to continue. Anyway, it seemed to be over."

"Any regrets? He doesn't sound like a dark, threatening person to me."

"No, he was a darling man and it was an experience I'll never forget, but he wasn't right for me. I must have been slightly mad to go off with him, though I never hesitated!"

When I left the session, my head was swirling with happy memories of barreling along endless deserted roads, occasionally passing a load of hay drawn by a slow tractor. After climbing over ancient ruins and taking pictures of each other, we would stop for the usual fare of feta cheese, olives and cucumbers, topping off the adventure with a bottle of the Turkish version of ouzo in the evening. The food wasn't memorable, with the exception of fresh fish now and then, but that didn't matter. I wouldn't have missed our escapades for the world.

As I continued to reflect, I realized that in those days I could never have been happy anchored to one place even if I had found an adoring husband. That was my nature. I was a free spirit in desperate need of adventure.

71

So why had Neil's departure hit me so hard? Was it that I was finally ready for a solid relationship, for something more meaningful? We'd had so much in common. I was more determined than ever to explore my feelings and to understand Neil's deceitfulness. What had gone wrong?

*   *   *

At the end of that session Byron had looked at me seriously and said, "I want you to sit down and go back over your life — your mother, art school, all of it, and try to tie it together, maybe even write down as much as you can remember."

PART IV

Reflections and Revelations

CHAPTER ELEVEN

As I pulled into my driveway, I felt hesitant about walking into the empty house and tried not to think of Neil. Every time I dwelt on losing him, I'd obsess over my feelings of abandonment and then get annoyed at myself. Taking a deep breath, I walked inside, made myself a cup of tea and sat in the living room with pen and paper trying to piece together my life.

When I graduated from college, all my friends were getting married, but I headed for New York. My mother said, "There are a lot more interesting things to do than getting married, dear." This was a relief since I hadn't yet fallen in love and didn't want to be stuck in some small town like my mother. I wanted to travel and meet exciting people in the arts.

So leaving my cello behind, I went off to New York unaware that few women there were accepted into the art world. Eager to study painting, I applied to Cooper Union Art School, passed the exam, and started classes feeling I had at last arrived home. I had certainly been the Green Monkey in college and in my hometown, always feeling like an outsider. Now in New York I felt a freedom to be whatever I chose.

There were people of all ages and backgrounds in the school, but we shared one great interest in common and that's all that seemed important. Naively I felt sure that studying here would lead to a career as an artist. Little did I realize I would spend years working as a gallery assistant.

My first year in New York was difficult – lonely and depressing. I timidly applied for a job in a museum, aware that I had few qualifications, and was pleased to be hired as a receptionist at a very low salary. Attending art school at night and working at the museum during the day left little time for anything else. Fortunately, I found a cheap basement apartment in Greenwich Village and, thrilled to have a place of my own, determined to make ends meet and carve out a life that was truly mine. My parents, I later learned, thought of this time as a little "fling", convinced I would eventually realize how tough life was in New York and go back home. So they left me on my own. Apparently they thought I was rebelling, but I never had that in mind; I was only trying to find my path.

Although college hadn't prepared me for anything practical, I knew how to type and I diligently studied speed writing at my reception desk in the museum. If I could get a job as a secretary, I figured it might lead to something interesting that would pay a better salary. My friends at art school worked as secretaries or teachers during the day and seemed to accept any job that enabled them to study at night. The business world was not very friendly toward single women, but none of us aspired to a future in business anyway.

Of the few women in art school, I made friends with two: Elida, a sweet, sensitive girl from Puerto Rico, and Gabe, an aggressive New Yorker who was outspoken and tough. They fascinated me. We had come from such different backgrounds, but now we were drawn together in the same pursuit. I never thought we would be lifelong friends, but they were part of this exciting new life in New York. We did not keep in touch after art school.

One thing we agreed on was that women were not taken seriously. But the fact that there were very few successful women artists didn't faze us. We were in our twenties and the future was of no concern! We lived for the present, assuming the future would one day take some form and shape.

On Saturdays, Elida, Gabe, and I would visit galleries uptown. There weren't many women artists in galleries, but one weekend Gabe said, "There's a show we've got to see at the Stable Gallery by a *woman,* and her work is really strong." That's when I first saw an exhibition of Joan Mitchell's paintings: wonderful abstractions with free brush strokes and brilliant color weaving in and out of a white ground. Her work had an intense energy, which to me was more like music than landscape. She became my idol. Reading books about her, I learned that she considered herself an outsider everywhere, an alien without an identity – clearly a Green Monkey! She strove to paint her private, or inner, landscape and from my perspective her paintings were very successful.

A few weeks later we saw Marisol's sculpture – whimsical and clever figures carved out of wood. Strongly influenced by her forms, I came across a pile of old oak beams from a demolished building and had them delivered to a studio I was subleasing on Fourteenth Street, a small space I could leave in a mess which was better than trying to work in my apartment. Right away I started sculpting, excited by the abstract shapes and colors in the wood grain itself. At night I would lug my sculptures to school on the bus for a critique by my teachers, hoping for encouragement. I now realize it was an attempt to find my individuality or the nature of the Green Monkey in me.

*   *   *

Nevertheless, despite my friendships with Elida and Gabe and my enthusiasm for my classes, I was depressed and finally decided to go to a therapist. I really didn't know why I was unhappy; I certainly wasn't homesick, and going home was no option anyway. I couldn't afford therapy, but there was no point in asking my parents to help pay for it. *Psychology* was a word you didn't mention in my family.

It was a tabu I first learned about during a weekend home from college with my good friend Terry, a grad student in psychology. As we were about to return to campus, I went out to the garden to say goodbye to my father, who turned to me and angrily stated that he never wanted me to see Terry again. I was stunned at my father's intensity, which was completely out of character. I asked why, but he wouldn't give me an explanation.

I could only assume that because Terry was a therapist, my father felt compelled to protect some secret about my mother. My grandmother often told me as a child that my mother wasn't well, but it wasn't something we ever discussed. By the time I arrived back at school, I was sure my father was trying to keep me from finding out about my mother's problems.

*   *   *

Staring into my teacup, I realized that even then she was, albeit unknowingly, sabotaging my chance at a relationship with an attractive man! I made myself another cup of tea and thought about the awful depression I had felt in New York.

Eventually I found a therapist who offered me a reduced rate through a clinic in midtown Manhattan. Her name was Mrs. McDermot. She was a bit intimidating and serious, but I began telling her about my life, not knowing where this was going. I told her I didn't understand why I was lonely and sad. Then it all started pouring out – experiences in my childhood that I had never before shared with anyone. I ended my first session by telling her a dream I'd had recently:

I'm a young child, about eight years old. I go to my aunt's house and, when she's not looking, I climb onto a chair to steal the honey in her cupboard.

Mrs. McDermot explained that since I couldn't get the sweetness and love at home, I tried to steal it from my aunt.

80

Actually my aunt's house next door had been a refuge from my mother's emotional outbursts. I laughed to myself thinking of my sweet aunt. She didn't like my mother and was always pleased to see me, since these visits annoyed my mother. My own interpretation of the dream came from an English movie I'd seen called *A Taste of Honey,* which was about a self-centered mother who neglected her daughter. Recalling how impossible it was for me to talk to my mother, I began to cry.

In time, Mrs. McDermot explained that my mother most likely had a borderline personality disorder and could probably be termed psychotic. As intrigued as I was by the word *borderline*, the description of this condition sounded scary, but surprisingly in accord with my mother's behavior. Mrs. McDermot said people with this disorder usually feel nothing for others, are extremely hypersensitive to criticism, and have problems getting close to others.

For months I dwelled on her interpretation, looking at my childhood through this lens. Although I had always known my mother as the highly sensitive person she believed herself to be, I began to realize she was only sensitive to herself. She certainly wasn't curious about how I felt, or anyone else for that matter. Whenever I'd try to tell her about incidents at school, she would stop me short with a curt phrase, such as, "That's nice, dear," or "You'll get over it." If I came home in tears, she would give me a piece of pie to make me feel better. She seemed to be somewhere else and uninterested in hearing about my life. I had to agree with Mrs. McDermot that my mother wasn't a healthy mirror for a child, and eventually I saw that she was at the root of my problems. Understanding this made me feel less guilty about my inability to get along with her. It also made me aware that I had been lonely *all* my life, even while living at home.

It occurred to me that I had always made an effort to portray myself as a normal person because I didn't think I was normal. Deep down, I now realized, this was because I had identified with my mother. In fact, I always felt there was probably something abnormal or unacceptable about me, and I had to put on a front so no one could see it. Obsessed with this new understanding, I began to wonder if I ever got away with this mask of normality or if others could see through it. My very being became a dichotomy, and I was never sure who the real *me* was. Too bad I didn't know about the Green Monkey at that stage of my life.

* * *

Still dealing with bouts of depression years later while living in Los Angeles, I went to another therapist, Nelson.

He was just out of grad school and someone I could relate to easily. Nelson repeatedly told me my depression was inherited from my mother – something I had realized for years, so it didn't change anything to hear this.

Several months after I began therapy with Nelson, my parents decided to visit me for Christmas, and I went to meet them at the airport. From a distance, I could see my mother wearing a long, flowing navy plaid cape and high heels. As she drew nearer, I could see she had on a blonde wig and bright red rouge.

"How do I look, dear?" she asked.

I was stunned. I couldn't say anything. Thoughts raced through my mind: she wants sympathy from me, she's putting on a distressed act to show how she suffers. Her drama always seemed artificial, but this time she had gone further. Now she wanted me to see how *disturbed* she was, and I wasn't sure if the act was real or not.

I told her she looked wonderful and drove them to a hotel. Then I dashed home to make an appointment with Nelson. As I walked into his office the next morning, I burst into uncontrollable tears. My mother had gone over the line, and there was no question how crazy she was!

He assured me that *she* was the psychotic person, not *me*. I looked at him in astonishment. Subconsciously, until then, I must have believed I was crazy, not just different or neurotic. Nelson stressed that I might be different and I might be feeling lost, but I was definitely *not* crazy. As I experienced this pain, I began to comprehend what Nelson had tried to explain to me over and over.

At last, aware that I was quite sane, I felt the depression lift, practically overnight. With it went a lot of my problems. In fact, I felt so much in touch with myself and my life that therapy no longer seemed necessary at that time. I was too busy dealing with the world to be unhappy.

*   *   *

A chill ran through my body as I relived that experience many years ago. I gulped down some of my tea, which was getting cold. The Green Monkey in me must have been behind the search for my sanity, although I was unaware of Green Monkeys in those days.

It wasn't until years later, when I came to Santa Fe and began therapy with Byron, that I began to look seriously at my history of relationships with men. He made me think about my attraction to the shadowy, distant, and emotionally unavailable lovers, and to question why I singled them out. There seemed to be a deeper level I needed to comprehend.

Now after today's session with Byron, I had other questions: Had I been avoiding serious relationships? Had

I put my painting first to prevent myself from getting involved in these entanglements that led nowhere? It was time to get more answers. As Byron put it: "We are constantly evacuating parts of our personality from the unconscious." There was more I needed to learn.

CHAPTER TWELVE

At our next session we went over what I had written, tying together a lot of loose ends. Then Byron encouraged me to look back at earlier relationships. Our sessions at this time dealt more with my past rather than dreams.

My thoughts raced back to my very first love, years ago in New York.   Tony was a tall, intense, dark-haired Spaniard, who was a respected artist among our peers. We had met the second year of art school and we had immediately recognized each other. The closeness we felt made it apparent that we had been soul mates in another lifetime. But this time it turned out to be a tumultuous affair that was very traumatic for me.

Nevertheless, there were things I had to learn from him, things that were important for the development of a "Green

Monkey", which I now realized had to do with awareness, questioning, finding answers, and building character.

I remember Tony saying to me once, "Never settle for less than the truth." We were young idealistic art students searching for some validity or meaning in life. Of course, it kept changing and we, or at least I was hardly prepared for that. One week he was sure he loved me and would spend days with me in my basement apartment. We would walk across Washington Square to school at night hand in hand, talking endlessly about painting. But the next week he would be in love with his wife, Lydia (who, in one of those amazing examples of synchronicity, had the same name as my mother!) Somehow emotions made finding the truth an elusive task. It was easier to find some validity in a canvas than to find answers in our lives.

Looking back, however, we did probe into dark corners, looking at our relationship, and trying to understand our feelings. We fought, questioning each other's motives and desires. I learned to search for solutions rather than accept the status quo. Probably this was because neither of us had a workable pattern to follow in our parents.

It wasn't ideal – actually a bad choice as he didn't want any commitments, but Tony made it impossible for me to deny what was going on between us. So why did I fall in love with him – a married man? I couldn't answer that. I think you just know when it happens, something inevitable.

Now, looking at Neil, I *realized* how remote he was in comparison to Tony. For a musician/composer, who grew up in the fairyland world of Hollywood, this approach to life must have seemed inconceivable. He pretended everything was just fine, and if I questioned his silences, he took it as an attack on his very being.

*   *   *

I recalled one night when I couldn't sleep thinking about us. I got up, poured myself a brandy and sat in the living room having a cigarette. Neil quietly appeared. I sensed him standing in the doorway.

Looking concerned and angry at the same time he asked, "What's wrong?"

I paused before saying, "Neil, you never want to discuss anything with me. I don't know what you're doing, how you feel about us or anything that's going on in your head."

He gave me a calm look, "I'm just involved in my work. That's the way I am. There's nothing wrong."

"Don't you realize how distant you are? Is it my imagination that we used to feel closer?" I puffed on my cigarette which, I'm sure, annoyed him.

He looked at me unemotionally, "Well, I think you're making up a problem. What do you want to know?"

"It doesn't matter how upset I am, you're not interested, are you?

"You're just trying to make me at fault."

"I'm only trying to talk to you!"

"Well, let's do it in the morning. I've got to get some sleep." He went back to bed. By now I was wide awake and frustrated and I couldn't hold back the tears.

He thought I was blaming him, when all I wanted was the freedom to explore our thoughts together. What was he hiding and why?

* * *

There is nothing as deadly as silence in a relationship. It was painful looking back at the end of the affair and recounting these events, but I was lost in reflection now. One day I was so upset that I called Nina to meet me for a drink at the Pink Adobe Bar. I remember we sat in front of the kiva fireplace eating popcorn and drinking margaritas.

She said, "OK, tell me about it. What's going on?"

I was on the verge of tears as I tried to explain, "I don't think Neil is in love with me anymore. There's this terrible distance. He's acting very mysterious. He watches television at night, doesn't talk to me, and often comes home late when I'm asleep."

She asked hesitantly, "Do you think there's someone else?"

It wasn't as though I hadn't considered it, but I said, "I don't think so, although he flirts with women and they seem to be attracted to him. But I don't think it goes beyond that." Was I trying to fool myself?

We decided to share a piece of the famous Pink Adobe apple pie with its special rum sauce. What could be better for depression than apple pie and margaritas?

I rambled on, "There was the time I waited for him at The Upper Crust. We were going to have a quick pizza before going to a movie at the Grand Illusion. He was so late that we had to forget the movie and he didn't really have any explanation. I don't know where he was or why he was late. He never even said he was sorry about it. Don't you think that's a bit strange?"

She looked at me with a concerned, puzzled expression and said, "If you and Neil would only sit down, have a few martinis and relax enough to laugh at yourselves, I think you could solve your problems. You always seem so perfect together! What you need is a sense of humor."

I nodded and replied, "You're absolutely right, but I can't get him to look at the problems. We seem to get side-tracked. He treats me like a child, joking about his work and friends, but it's not about us. I end up feeling as though I've been abandoned."

That conversation wasn't long before the end. I could already see it coming.

CHAPTER THIRTEEN

It amazes me now as I remember how the mystery seemed to unravel within a short time – in a dream:

There is a trial going on and I'm backstage with Neil, the defendant, who is expecting to be freed. He has a tux hanging there intending to go to a party when the trial is over. Three of us are asked to put on size-ten dresses to prove the victim wore a size-ten not a twelve. They are cheap dresses from K-Mart, but I actually like the one I try on.

In the end, the defendant is convicted to his surprise. I'm watching two cats running around. One looks a lot like my cat. The other is a black kitten and I think about keeping them.

Byron said, "Sounds like he thinks he's bulletproof. No one has a better facade than Neil. But he doesn't get away with it this time! It's about what I refer to as the Facade Animus. These are people who live with a facade. They've never wanted to look at the real self."

"Oh," I admitted, "I've known quite a few of those! A charming facade works well in dealing with the world."

"That's part of what you were attracted to in Neil. But it isn't the real person; it's like a shell. When you try to dig deeper to find the real feelings and values, you can't get through it."

I broke in, "There were so many times I tried to discuss my feelings and our relationship, but he made me feel I was being paranoid. He kept saying everything was just fine with him."

"He was hiding the real person, not wanting you to see that he was a phony, not *knowing* who he was. It's a result of childhood shame." He looked at me for my reaction.

"I could never succeed in developing a strong facade. Oh, I pretended to be OK, happy, whatever, but it didn't quite work. I didn't have the confidence inside to pull it off."

Byron smiled, "Green Monkeys aren't good at artificial facades." Then he went on seriously, "And the confidence?

93

You weren't given self-worth as a child. Reality for a child is contact." He paused. "In some ways my childhood was similar to yours and I can understand what you went through." Then he looked very thoughtful, adding, "We were wired backwards as children and learned negative states as love."

I knew what he meant and nodded. "But in the dream, he isn't going to get away with the facade this time?"

"Your psyche isn't going to let him get away with it this time. It's a progression from the stage male, and he's not going to walk like O.J. It's a healthy resolution."

I asked, "What about the size-ten dress from K-Mart?"

"Size-ten is smaller, probably more attractive to men than size-twelve, and it's a simple garment away from the illusions of Hollywood – getting more grounded. K-Mart is the common people."

"You haven't said anything about the cats."

"The transition to the kitties. Animals often represent feelings. No one has less feeling than Neil when it comes to you. Classic narcissistic wounds in his case. But the dream ends with real feelings in the animals."

He looked at me pushing up his glasses, and decided to go on explaining. "OK, let's look at the Facade Animus. He thinks he can get away with it. When two people meet, it's a re-union of two souls who have known each other before – a re-cognition of a past connection. You don't see the facade at first, but as the shell is peeled away and the unhealed child is revealed, then he can't get away with the facade any longer. It dissolves."

"I never wanted to see the facade, did I?"

"For a long time, we think there's a whole person in there, but it's really only a facade. He is afraid to reveal the real feelings of pain and hostility underneath, so he becomes unavailable."

I asked, "So that's the remoteness I feel?"

He nodded. "He withdraws. Intimacy is seen as a danger to him because the child never was able to trust. He expects to be smashed and hurt, so he'd better run. You can't have a mature relationship until the child is healed."

I commented, "So he really is acting like a child? No wonder I couldn't talk to him."

"The real person has been hidden for so long that it seems far easier for him to break up and wait to fall in love again, than to work his way toward a deeper relationship and to deal with the child within." Byron looked at me for a reaction before continuing, "He doesn't want to look at the real self. The damaged child feels he's got to be free, he's suffocating and must escape from the connection. He becomes the Flying Boy."

I frowned. "The what?" I asked.

Byron sighed, "They fly away – from commitments, feeling, responsibilities, intimacy…. Just when you think things are beginning to work out and the relationship is starting to gel, they fly in pursuit of another city, job, adventure, lover."

"That's Neil, isn't it?"

Byron just nodded.

*   *   *

That's what had happened with Neil. Everything began to make sense. The explanation of the Flying Boy gave me a clearer understanding of many of the men I had known. It was the same as the so-called Peter Pan Syndrome, but I liked Byron's term, Flying Boys. It seemed appropriate.

I went home from that session understanding more, but not knowing how to change anything, or even if there was a possibility of changing our lives.

We were invited to a party that evening given by a screenwriter we knew and I was glad to be going out. Neil was anxious to see some of the local film people who would be there, so he was in a good mood. I ran into some friends and the party turned into be a pleasant diversion that took my mind off Flying Boys.

Later, I noticed Neil talking to a very expressive young blonde who was flirting with him. She was so outrageous that I was getting a kick out of it. He seemed amused and flattered. As we drove home he seemed happy, more like the old Neil who could be so much fun.

A few days after the party, he mentioned that the girl kept calling him. I don't think I even felt any jealousy. She had seemed so flaky and young that I never dreamed he would fall for someone like her.

Well, he did. It was about two weeks later that he left. Byron claimed it wasn't the girl. Neil was just ready to run. When he left, he denied there was anyone else and I believed him. I thought he just needed to be alone to think things out for a time, but he never came back.

PART V

It Begins to Unravel…

CHAPTER FOURTEEN

During my last few sessions with Byron, I had come to a better understanding of myself and the years I spent with Neil. I also realized I had changed since he left.

That first year alone had been difficult. I spent a lot of time traveling in Mexico, Switzerland and, more recently, the Caribbean. Lying on a beach in Mexico, drinking margaritas and pina coladas, had been soothing in the balmy, lazy climate. Then I had gone to Gstadd to ski with a friend. The thing I love about skiing is that you are so caught up with the beauty of the mountains and trying to stay on your feet while taking it all in, that you have no time to think.

Often when I was feeling confused and depressed about Neil, I would sneak up the mountain for an afternoon of skiing. I'd come home exhilarated and better for the moment. A psychic once told me I get bored with depression so I find ways to get myself out of it, like skiing.

A few months ago, Nina asked me to take a Caribbean cruise with her. Actually, Nina convinced me I needed to get away and meet new men to forget about Neil. It was meant to be a fun-filled adventure to escape the depression and sadness I was still feeling. But such trips are never what you anticipate. Probably all that one should expect is new vistas and a reprieve from one's normal life.

We both felt a bit depressed when we got back. Typical of cruises, we hadn't met many interesting people and there were no single men. Nina is a gregarious blonde with hair to her waist, large blue eyes and a lot of energy, and she seldom has any problem socializing. Yet even she admitted that there weren't any people she had felt drawn to. I felt better when my friend, Liz, who talks to everyone, even your answering machine, said she hated cruises because she never found very attractive people on them.

I spoke to Byron about the depression when we returned. He thought it was the disconnection I had experienced during the week on the ship. Oh, yes, "disconnection" – something I had experienced a lot in the past few years with Neil.

Byron looked intense as he asked, "When are you going to express some of that anger you're feeling?"

I hadn't admitted how angry I was or how desperate I felt waking up some mornings. But now, months later, those feelings started to emerge, erupting at unexpected times – irrational anger at Byron and friends, anger that was disconnected to what was happening in my life. But I began to feel much more alive.

After the trip I decided that running away was no solution and it was time to start living my life again. I read more Jung and found that he had written a book on synchronicity. In fact, he had coined the term to designate the meaningful coincidence of unrelated events. Of course, I had to read that. He casually said he was inclined to accept chance when it came his way.

I began looking for chance coincidences in search of a new direction for my life. I found them, observed what they meant to me, and often discovered that they led me in the right direction. I remembered the time I accidentally dropped my resume when applying for a job at MGM. Rather than look at my resume, they had insisted I fill out their numerous job applications and take a typing test. I never bothered to complete their application, as I had a feeling it would only go into a dead file of applicants. But the next day I had a call from someone I had met at a film shoot, saying he was surprised to find my resume on his desk. He asked me if I was looking for a job and suggested an opening in the story department. I started working there the following week.

Sometimes the synchronicity of events brought valuable opportunities to me. I also read that synchronicity tends to happen when it is needed.

I realized I was feeling stronger and one night I went to a gallery opening alone to see the sculpture of Jesús Moroles. I found myself staring at a large marble piece and right through it to a brightly colored embroidered vest. My eyes went up and saw that it was Tim Rutledge, a sculptor whom Neil had known. We both laughed as our eyes met and he asked, "Hey, how are you doing? I heard that Neil went back to LA."

"I'm doing OK. I don't think it could ever have worked with Neil."

Tim was big and rugged looking with a nice smile. We talked for awhile and then he said, "Why don't we have dinner some night?"

I said I'd love to and we made a date. He was attractive and someone I'd like to know better.

*   *   *

Last night I had another dream about Neil. He appears in my dreams constantly. Sometimes I shut them off and can't remember any for weeks, then he reappears. For the past few months he never speaks in them, but then, as Byron pointed out, Neil never was in touch with himself or anyone. The real Neil remained hidden. In the dream last night, we're in Los Angeles:

I meet Neil at a friend's house to sign some papers. He signs them and leaves without a word. His young girlfriend stays behind at the dinner party. This is convenient as it gives me a chance to observe her. I see her in a different light than when I first saw her at the party. In the dream, she wanders aimlessly, acting as though she is accustomed to being left in strange places. I don't know where Neil has gone or why he has left her with us.

Then, suddenly, I'm back in Santa Fe in my own garden (my unconscious, according to Byron). The garden is very overgrown. I realize I haven't cultivated it during the time I spent with Neil. Now I recognize it as a shadow garden with unknown areas to explore. I find a guest house that has been unused for years and I'm excited about fixing it up. The living room is full of Indian rugs and Kilims in wonderful colors and I start to rearrange them. My guest house is full of life!

I awoke in a good mood thinking of the expensive rugs! The dream indicated that I should explore myself and see the bright colors. There seemed to be a lot of potential in it and, possibly, an exciting future.

I wanted to hear Byron's interpretation of the dream. He always came up with surprising revelations that I didn't see. I called him and he said he had a free hour in the afternoon.

When I told him the dream, he laughed and said, "The young blonde girl is you. You're observing your shadow side. With these guys – all your life – you played the non-savvy little anima chick on some level – subservient, long suffering, glossing over: 'It's OK. Men are like that. That's what they want.' This is you in this dream!"

I was startled at this revelation and objected to his accusation, "I never identified with that role at all. I never even thought I was very attractive and I *wasn't* a dumb blonde ..."

"Of course you didn't see it. But you unconsciously played it to the hilt with blinders on, because you're attractive and blonde. It's a role of denial. We all do this at times. No blame. The wounded child learns to play a role – not self, an archetype, one sided. It's so limited. That's what you were given. Painful, isn't it?" I must have made an awful face, because he went on in peals of laughter. "Your shadow is a dumb blonde. You weren't dumb, but you weren't using your faculties. This isn't personal. That's what certain gentlemen, most of them, want."

"I know," I said, "I see it all the time. They are comfortable with the subservient, dumb blonde type."

Byron nodded, "No shit, Sherlock."

*   *   *

On my way home from Byron's office I tried to look at why Neil had left. I thought the karma I had with Neil meant we were destined to be together. But, oh no! Now I tried to understand it and found many lessons that I had learned from being with him. I also saw numerous flaws in myself.

Maybe I had unconsciously resorted to the dumb blonde image which was non-threatening. Neil loved to be the center of attention. He was entertaining and liked to tell stories. I suppose I was intimidated, and not wanting to compete with him or risk confrontation, I stayed in the background.

When I studied the situation I saw that I was always busy cooking and giving dinner parties. Much of the time I didn't get into the conversation. Once Neil asked me my opinion of a subject as I was bringing some drinks out to the deck. I hadn't heard any of the discussion, so I could hardly comment. Most of the time he wasn't interested in my opinion and I was annoyed that he chose that time to ask me what I thought. Without knowing, I was fading into the background.

The irony of it was that I had always thought of myself as very independent. It was difficult for me to lean on a man or to be dependent in any sense. By now I felt that I had become a strong woman, quite capable and successful in my work – perhaps I appeared too strong at times to appeal to men.

That was probably the very reason I had faded into the background. I felt I had to be subservient to appeal to Neil. My God, how we sacrifice Self to get love!

CHAPTER FIFTEEN

July 4th has often been an eventful date for me. I first arrived in Santa Fe twelve years ago, on a 4th of July, during an eclipse of the moon at midnight with an ailing Peugeot, piled high with my belongings. The car was barely moving and we had come about 500 miles at 45 miles an hour – no garage in the desert would look at a French car. A friend had driven with me. Although we started out with high expectations, by now our anticipation of arriving in Santa Fe had dimmed and we were just exhausted.

My cat, Heathcliff, had been hiding all day under piles of stuff in the back. I wasn't even sure if he was still alive until we went over La Bajada Hill and the lights of Santa Fe appeared in the distance. Somehow my wonderful

Heathcliff knew and crawled up onto the seat to look out the window. He knew we had arrived.

*   *   *

Now so many years later, I was celebrating the Fourth of July again with Tim, the sculptor. I've been seeing him for a few months and he has been very supportive in helping me through the trauma of the past year. It occurs to me it has been five years, almost to the day, since Neil first came to Santa Fe and I fell in love with him.

As I observed Tim, I thought how attractive he was – tall with lots of dark hair, and he looks marvelous in a black Western hat along with his usual jeans and cowboy boots. He always walks as though his feet hurt in the boots, but that seems to go along with the romantic cowboy image. Inside he's just a great big puppy dog.

Tim broke up with Lita a few months before my breakup with Neil. She was a tall, thin girl with long dark hair – his perfect counterpart, but Lita didn't survive his dogmatic ways for long. Tim never understood, although she wrote letters explaining her departure. He thought she was very neurotic and had a lot of problems which explained the breakup. Obviously he didn't want to look deeper. Fortunately, I never got into that kind of relationship with Tim, so I never completely understood why she had left. I could see the many pitfalls and we never became more than close, commiserating friends.

I'd had a somewhat disturbing session with Byron that day which was still rummaging around in my mind. I often had vivid dreams the night before our sessions, and the previous night Tim had been in my dream. As I recalled my discussion with Byron, I thought of telling Tim about it.

Before I mentioned the dream, I said to Byron, "You know Tim's only a friend, but he can be so warm and caring. Sometimes it brings tears to my eyes and it's confusing because I don't know that I feel anything for him, or that I could care about anyone just now."

Byron had a way of ruminating on all the data he had and sizing up my frame of mind before coming up with a long explanation: "It's your massive lifelong deprivation, emotional starvation. We've got to get the girl (the Inner Child) out of the tower so she can feel, get what's appropriate and what the heck is true! Truth is what you feel, not what you think. You can't cut yourself off from feeling all this. Acknowledge the whole thing. No one was ever emotionally present for you. Now you attain the truth through these tears. You must allow the connection rather than hard edge denial and bucking up – examine it as it swirls around. You were in the background with Neil. Now you're coming to the foreground."

I smiled in recognition of what he was saying, but I also realized I could have blown it if I hadn't stayed in the background. Neil certainly didn't want competition.

Then I told Byron about my disturbing dream:

Tim and I find two bodies and a lot of blood. They are in a closet. We didn't kill them, but we're trying to cover it up. If anyone finds out, they will probably think we're guilty.

Byron roared in his bombastic way and looked at me over his glasses. "Is this a stretch? His girlfriend, your boyfriend. Come on." He could always see the irony and humor in dreams, which made them seem lighter and more acceptable.

"But they were very young in this dream," I said. "Two young bodies and very gory!"

He looked serious now as he said, "Well, I think there's a lot to it. I think Neil is very young emotionally and he's very bloodied. People fixate on the family of origin to try to solve the problem. I don't think it's a far fetched dream at all."

I gave him a very puzzled look.

He tried to explain, "OK, when a child never received the love he needed, to him 'love' means hurt and pain. Then as an adult, he unconsciously kills love because he never experienced success in relationships or love. He reenacts the hurt and pain later in life, destroying potential relationships. Again, I repeat, he can't love until the Inner Child is healed."

I asked, "How does the Inner Child get healed?"

"Well, look at you – long suffering, nearly paralyzed as a child. When you move towards awareness, a transformation takes place and you can say no to the dysfunctional type of relationship. The ability to have long term, stable relationships was really murdered in Neil as a child."

"And there was nothing I could do to change that?"

"The question of being found guilty," he mused. "How much responsibility do you bear in this failed relationship? Probably none."

"I feel like I failed at *something*, and maybe that's a lot of why I worry about being found guilty in the dream."

I felt impatient as it had been over a year now that I'd been trying to sort this out, and it seemed to be taking forever to resolve these problems.

113

"But nobody can make it work until he chooses to. It takes will. See, you've got a lot of will. He didn't want to be a crazy person – that's one of the reasons he was with you, a refuge from his own insanity."

"Then why couldn't it have worked for him?"

"He's too addicted to the old pattern."

"I think maybe it was the first time I really wanted to make a relationship work."

"Part of that is your developing maturity and part your karma with Neil. That's called love. You had many past lives with him that weren't resolved. Worthy of tears. See, I don't have a problem with tears. Tears don't mean you're not fine. They're an expression of your truth, your feelings, including the love that shattered here. Your dreams are looking at it."

I smiled as I realized how Byron never tried to mask the truth to make it easier to accept. Every session added to the picture to make it a clearer whole.

* * *

I started to tell Tim about the session with Byron as we relaxed over drinks on his patio. His house was in Arroyo Hondo outside Santa Fe, but it felt like a Mexican hacienda with old wooden doors and saltillo tiles throughout. We watched the sunset behind the mountains way in the distance, as the sky became scarlet and purple.

Tim listened to me as he barbecued hamburgers. Then he came over and put his arm around me and said, "I think it's time you had some fun, and we're going to see some good fireworks tonight!" And maybe that's just what I needed. Obviously he didn't want to get into a serious conversation that could be uncomfortable. This was typical. I should have known. I began to understand why Lita had left. He didn't want to understand her feelings or needs.

After we finished eating, we got in his big truck and went off to the middle of a mesa where his friend lived. When we arrived, Alan was showing photographs on a screen set up outside his studio. Many were of magnificent New Mexico skies and clouds. I looked up at the vast space above us with millions of bright stars. Tim went to work behind the screen, preparing the fireworks. He loved fireworks – just a kid really – and it all had a great sense of celebration. Maybe this was the true end to the Neil affair. My sadness seemed to be in the past. I was feeling really good as Tim's missiles noisily zoomed everywhere. Off to the left you could see the city fireworks, while in the distance, there were other displays; and way off to the right

Fredericka Heller

was the best show of all as the sky was lit by summer lightning.

Driving back to Tim's house, I felt happy and alive. I hugged him, said goodnight and drove home. I knew I didn't want any relationship with Tim, and I had no regrets that I was no longer with Neil. Tim seemed surprised at my abrupt departure, but it was the appropriate end to the evening, and I saw no reason to make excuses about why I intended to go home.

PART VI

A Time to Act

CHAPTER SIXTEEN

It was the day after Tim's fireworks that I received a call for Neil from a bank in Albuquerque. I explained to a hostile voice that he wasn't living here anymore. I had a dreadful feeling it was about the Toyota truck we purchased together.

She said, "Yes, it is about a Toyota truck. Who are you?" I gave her my name and there was a silence.

Then she found me – still listed as co-owner. Apparently I had been lost in the file and all of the correspondence was going to Neil's old P.O. Box. She told me they were threatening to repossess the truck as he had not been making payments. There seemed to be no end to this involvement, for it had been nearly a year since I'd seen or talked to Neil. I said I would go down to Albuquerque the next day to discuss the problem with her.

Something told me I'd better call the insurance company, too. I had a nervous feeling in the pit of my stomach that said "listen to your intuition". I was right. They had canceled the insurance six months ago! Again, it seems all correspondence had gone to a P.O. Box and my name, in effect, was all but deleted from the file. I was suddenly feeling a nervous wreck, weak in the knees and vulnerable. This couldn't be happening. He needed the truck. Why was he being so irresponsible? Was he broke?

When Neil left, Byron told me to pack up his belongings and put them in storage. "Deal with all of it. Get everything out of your house – clean slate. And what about the truck and credit cards?" I didn't want to even think about it at that point.

But I hadn't realized I was in serious jeopardy. I made some calls and found out that if the truck were repossessed, it would ruin my credit for the next seven years. Seven years!

Worse than that, I could be sued if he were in a wreck. They wouldn't go after him – obviously he couldn't even afford the payments. I would be the target. And over

$5000 was still owing on the truck. How could he drive in Los Angeles without insurance? Now I was angry.

I had been such a sucker! Neil was in a bad wreck with his new girlfriend just two weeks after he left me. (Could it be retribution?) He came by to get the insurance papers and a neck pillow, and told me the gory details. Luckily they had been wearing seat belts, as the car was demolished and they were taken to hospital. Obviously he was still in pain.

He said he'd like to keep the Toyota and take over the payments, which I had been making. I really didn't want the stupid truck with a stick shift that always clunked when I drove it, and I didn't want anything that reminded me of Neil, so I agreed he could take the Toyota.

I guess I also felt sorry for him and still cared about him deep down somewhere. His car was gone and he was stuck with a helpless girl with broken ribs. Later, I often speculated who got stuck with whom? I'm sure she thought he was a very successful composer more than willing to take care of a beautiful, young, adoring girl. After all, "she had always lived with older men," as I later learned.

* * *

Fearfully, I drove down to Albuquerque the next morning and went to the bank that carried the loan on the truck. I entered the main branch, but was told that the

Repossession Department had been moved, and I was sent to a basement office in another building. There were women at every desk. I was ushered into the office of the Director of the department whose name was Beth. To my surprise, she was very sympathetic. Obviously, she had dealt with this sort of situation before with a number of women, and none of it was new to her.

I tried to explain my situation to her: "Even if I make the delinquent payments and get the truck back, I couldn't sell it because it's in both our names."

As she looked through the file, I thought of a possible solution and said, "Why don't we let them repossess it? Then I will go to Los Angeles, pay off the loan and at least I'll have possession."

Beth looked distracted as she sorted through her file and said, "No, that won't work, it would still ruin your credit." She looked up at me, "And in California, all you have to do is make the two delinquent payments and you're reinstated. He might find a way to do this as soon as it's actually repossessed." She rummaged through more papers in silence, then she turned to me and smiled, "You know what? It's in your name OR Neil's name."

The light dawned, "You mean if I could somehow get the truck before they repossessed it, I could sell it without his signature?" I felt a wave of relief float over me. Yet, just the thought of it made me nervous.

She answered with a sly grin, "If you were to go out to Los Angeles and drive the truck away, it would be perfectly legal."

I was a bit stunned, but slowly the light dawned on me and I asked, "That's what you're suggesting?" I didn't have any guts when it came to that sort of thing. She implied she might even be able to get me a code to have a key made!

I pondered over the whole situation as I drove home, gazing at the mountains in the distance. I was always enchanted by the red glow as the sun set on the Sangre de Cristo Mountains.

By the time I pulled into my driveway, I had decided to call my friend, Zane, a dropout whiz of an attorney. Briefly I told him the whole story, and he said he'd be right over.

He analyzed the whole mess from a legal point of view, making it sound even more crucial than I had thought. We sat outside drinking gin and tonic, ruminating over the whole situation. I asked Zane, "Why would he let the insurance run out and not tell me?"

He laughed at my naivete and asked, "If you have nothing to lose, what does it matter? He's doing the LA two step – talk, talk, talk... Remember Neil? He never looked you in the eye, somewhere to the side of you. They probably raised the insurance rate after he demolished the car or they refused to insure him." Zane tended to be a bit fatalistic and negative, not much faith in human nature.

That got to me and I started to get angry at the whole mess I had gotten into. We both sat there, silently staring at the pool trying to figure out what to do. He was being very objective. At least it felt good to have his support at this point.

I said, "Another gin?"

He said, "Yeah."

When I came back with the drinks, he looked at me and said, "Let's go get it." Just like that.

I said, "Go steal it?"

He said, "Yeah."

I wasn't at all sure I wanted to do that and I didn't know if he was serious. I wondered why he was offering to help me. He had been Neil's friend as well as mine, and he was the type who only told you about a quarter of what was revolving around in his mind. Yet I felt I could trust him. He was smiling to himself now in deep thought. When he finished his drink, he got up to leave saying, "Think it over. I'll call you tomorrow."

CHAPTER SEVENTEEN

The next morning, I awoke in a frenzy. The whole nightmare came back slowly as I came out of another disturbing dream:

I'm in an earthquake, swept into water along with some young girls. Everything is being washed away and falling. We expect to drown, but suddenly we're swept out of a tunnel and into a building. I find myself in an apartment high above the water, watching the levies being swept away. We seem to be safe, but we don't know what is happening in the outside world. I feel like I'm high in an ivory tower, as I had often been as a young girl, escaping trauma!

I thought of what Byron had said, "It's time to get out of the tower and get what's appropriate in your life..."

As I slipped back into reality, I realized I had to decide what to do and fast – get out of the tower, get going! I stumbled out of bed and grabbed some old Levis and a shirt. I wasn't quite sure I wanted to go to California with Zane. After I made some coffee, I decided to call a friend in LA and ask him if he could help me get the truck. He was an out-of-work actor and said sure, he could help me. Then he started thinking of himself as Sam Spade – he even knew a PI in his therapy group, if we couldn't pull it off.

While I was trying to make a decision, I decided to get some odd jobs done to get my mind off the dilemma. It was one of those days. I'd been meaning to paint the numbers on my mailbox in bright red so people could see my address, and I headed outside with the paint. I was mulling over everything and suddenly realized I was spilling red paint on my shoes and all over the pavement. I rushed inside to find the paint thinner, leaving drips along the way.

When I came out to mop up the paint, I was approached by two Jehovah's Witnesses and there was no escape. They could see what a mess I was in, but one of them was undaunted. She stared at me, asking, "Have you ever wondered why we don't live longer when we know our cells are replaced constantly? Turtles can live for 200 years!"

My telephone rang and I gladly raced into the house, but too late to catch whoever was calling – probably Zane. I wasn't sure what to tell him yet. One of the women had followed me to the front door and when I returned, she pointed out some red paint on the door latch, as she went right on about the cells and aging.

I must have looked distressed, because she finally handed me two pamphlets and said, "Dear, I'll come back when you're not so busy. But I think you'll enjoy these."

That afternoon all sorts of synchronistic events started to occur. My flaky friend, Liz, arrived with a young girl to swim just as my phone started ringing. She overheard me talking to Beth about getting the code to make a key for the truck. Of course, I had to tell her the whole story. She volunteered to be my accomplice. She said she loved that sort of thing and I gave it some serious thought.

Liz was an old friend I had met in New York years ago – the last person I ever expected to turn up in Santa Fe. Even though she was seventy-two she looked great, openly admitting to a number of facelifts. She was tall with reddish hair and had always been stunning. She loved Santa Fe as no one here considered her eccentric or crazy.

It occurred to me that I knew a lot of eccentric women, or as some would say flaky or nutty. Now I knew why.

127

They attracted me like the shadow men in my life. I felt at home with the oddballs as they were familiar, like my mother. I also knew a number of older women who were mother figures in a sense, but more the type I could relate to, in contrast to my own mother. Maybe I was subconsciously trying to find a mother to mirror – one that I liked.

Now Liz went on to explain that she had dealt with four divorces, which gave her a good background for this kind of thing. She certainly had guts and I admired that. I could just see it, though, a sort of Thelma and Louise saga crossing the desert with Liz. No, it wouldn't work. But then her friend said she would be glad to house-sit for me and things started falling together.

After they left, I went into the house and collapsed on a couch. I was in no frame of mind to do anything today. Zane kept coming to mind. In the end I opted for Zane.

I called him to see when he could leave. He said tomorrow. He was dead serious about getting the truck – fast.

*   *   *

I was suddenly feeling a sense of urgency. The repossession letter had already been sent out. Byron had been telling me over and over to deal with the truck, to clean up the remaining link with Neil. I didn't want to think about it. Now I had to. I changed my clothes and dashed down to get some airline tickets for the following night. I got a key made from the code Beth had given me. Then I went to our insurance company. It was becoming an adventure and I was beginning to feel bolder.

Neil had originally taken out insurance on the truck from his insurance company, but when they found out we weren't married, they had canceled! It seemed ridiculous and I never did understand why we couldn't own a truck together. For some reason I can't remember, *my* company wouldn't insure us either at that time. We finally found another company that would insure the truck, but only if I insured my house with them, which seemed to be our only alternative.

Now I decided to go in and speak to the manager about reinsuring the Toyota. He looked at me coldly, as he told me they were still paying medical bills and flatly refused to insure the truck again. He wasn't at all friendly or helpful, so I headed for my old insurance company.

Things started going in my favor. I walked in and told Lena I wanted to insure a truck as well as my car which they insured. She got the forms out as we discussed her two-inch nails and her daughters, who had both moved back home with their babies. I signed and left with the truck insured in both names (just in case we didn't retrieve it).

I started thinking about Neil. I still couldn't imagine why he would ever drive in Los Angeles without insurance after his wreck. What if he were badly hurt in another wreck? Possibly he couldn't get any insurance. Then it occurred to me that Neil was counting on my cowardice, thinking I would receive the cancellation notice and insure the truck. I had been the one who always took care of such matters. After all, he had nothing to lose but his life. That was Neil – always counting on his Guardian Angels to come up with miracles. But I knew they weren't always around when he needed them to get him out of a jam.

Now that it was becoming a reality, I started getting nervous. Why had I ever gotten into such a relationship?

I went to the library to get books-on-tape for the trip back across the desert – that was being optimistic!

CHAPTER EIGHTEEN

As I drove home I reminisced more about Neil. And I had thought he was so right for me! I remembered an article about Gloria Steinem in *Vanity Fair*. The interviewer asked Gloria about a much-publicized romance and Gloria asked her if she had ever been in love with someone who was totally inappropriate.

The interviewer responded that she had never been in love with any other kind! So why not relax and enjoy it! That rang a familiar note. Then I read Gloria Steinem's book, *Revolution from Within*.

I've always admired Gloria Steinem and identified with her, as I'm sure half my generation did. As I read her book, I noted many similarities in our lives. Although I had never been an active feminist, I had unknowingly led my life as one.

My mother, of course, like hers, was never a "mother type." She had given up an exciting career to marry my father, after divorcing a music critic – something you didn't talk about in those days, so I never learned much about him. She had been on the stage in the twenties and traveled back and forth to Europe during an era that was romantic and elegant. Now I realized (after some input from Byron) that she was a Flying Girl, not wanting to come down to earth. That's why she was so erratic!

I'm sure her fantasy, like any Flying Girl's, was to marry my father and live a settled life in the country with children, entertain her New York friends at their country home, and have an adoring man to take care of her.

Actually, she achieved her fantasy, but she was bored to death. She missed the glamorous life she had loved. In this new life, as a housewife and mother, she sank into terrible depressions. Her angry tantrums were frightening to a child, so I withdrew from her. I was supposed to make her happy, but I didn't. I was to blame for being quiet instead of an entertaining and loving child. (I wasn't aware of any of this until I grew up.)

I often wondered why she had married my father. He never seemed able to stand up to my mother. Eventually I saw that my father represented safety for her – safety from the inner turmoil that caused her frustrated outbursts, created by the "demon of her crazy animus" (her wounded male side derived from her own experience with men, as Byron had explained it). My father's perceived stability was something she needed as a hideout for her inner unsafety. Nevertheless, she lashed out at him, needing someone to blame. I'm sure his remoteness was infuriating to her, and yet, I could see it was the only way he knew to respond.

* * *

One summer my college boyfriend, Jamie, came to visit. After consuming a few beers late in the evening, he accurately summed up my parents, saying, "Your mother is always on the stage and your father is asleep in the audience." Jamie was the first intellectual I had ever met and I, too, had found a comfortable escape into the world of ideas at that point in my life.

Looking back, I realized that being an only child, I was left pretty much adrift, given little direction to deal with the world out there. I was brought up under the old dictum: "Children are to be seen and not heard" – and probably the less seen the better. I often wondered where I got my values; I think they were intuitive and logical, having spent a lot of time alone. They had nothing much to do with the real world. I seemed to use the phrase "in reality" a lot. I must have meant in the world out there as opposed to my interior world. I could never stand up to my mother and certainly not compete with her. She dominated the family like a spoiled, demanding child and we all tried to please her. She was the diva. My uncle once called her Madame Callas, as he stormed out of the house.

Something was missing in our family. Now, years later, I realized that something had to do with warmth and love which, of course, had a lot to do with my failure in relationships.

Having survived those days of growing up in my family, I see why I became extremely independent. I valued my freedom more than anything. I didn't want to depend on anyone for anything. Actually I must have been afraid to trust anyone. I have to admit I did get "pinned" to my intellectual boyfriend, Jamie, while in college. But I don't think it meant marriage or commitment to me. I had my first memorable dream the night I got pinned:

I nearly drive off a cliff. I manage to stop the car in time, but I'm terrified.

When I awoke the next morning, I couldn't wait to give back the pin. But I had to wait for two weeks as the fraternity was scheduled to serenade me, and I didn't have the nerve to back out so fast.

When it came down to it, I always knew I couldn't live my life for a man. I could never be "owned." There wasn't any choice but to live it my way. But relationships were important. This became a dilemma. We all need love and it doesn't help to deny it. Now, looking at my relationship with Neil, I realized how difficult it was to maintain a separate identity. I guess I must have intuitively known this all my life.

I also saw how an emotional involvement could change everything. It was worse than an obsession, like an addiction. I had begun to feel it was the only important thing in life – even though it was in conflict with all of my values.

*   *   *

With Byron's help, I looked at the whole pattern of my life and it began to fall together like a puzzle I had never completed.

Byron referred to my mother as narcissistic, entirely self-absorbed, interested only in her appearance and the impression she made on others. He pointed out that she was

135

never available. She was off in her unconscious in her desperate search for survival – a child herself in many ways, not adult enough to give anything to a child.

"A child tries to identify with damaged parents, but can't," he explained. "You had to be the adult. Your mother had a psychotic animus which you picked up as the pattern for men you attracted all your life." Now it became apparent that what I found in men was the same instability my mother constantly suffered.

My life had become a search for love, whatever that was – the missing element in my life! My mother, who resembled Bette Davis, would tell me in her booming Welsh accent, "you know we love you, dear." But there didn't seem to be much warmth or sincerity in that statement which I saw as contradictory to her critical behavior. I sensed the craziness of her psyche even before Byron referred to her "psychotic animus." So, when I found these qualities in a man, something deep inside unconsciously went for it, thinking "That's love!" – the more neurotic the better, just like my mother.

I was stunned to find an accurate description of this pattern in Jung's book: *Four Archetypes* (collected works of C.G. Jung, vol. 9,i) It was in a chapter on the mother complex and I immediately saw that I fell into the category entitled "Resistance to the Mother" (which for me was a matter of self-preservation).

Jung states:

> "This kind of daughter knows what she does not want, but is usually completely at sea as to what she would choose as her own fate. All her instincts are concentrated on the mother in the negative form of resistance, and are, therefore, of no use to her in building her own life. Should she get as far as marrying, either marriage will be used to the sole purpose of escaping from her mother, or a diabolical fate will present her with a husband who shares all the essential traits of her mother's character."

Well, I kept finding men who unwittingly had many of my mother's qualities, but some sense of sanity must have kept me from marrying them!

I had spent my life looking for a man who wasn't "inappropriate." So I had never married. Family life wasn't at all appealing to me – I had experienced enough of that as a child. Maybe I was like my mother and feared marriage would bore me. And I never had a great desire to have children, certainly not with the writers and artists I knew, who were insecure and non-committal. They also viewed

137

me as competition. I never knew this when I was younger, as I was unaware that they weren't looking for their intellectual equal as I was.

I suppose they saw me as a dumb blonde and didn't want to look deeper. What did I see in them? Was I so desperate not to be alone? Was that me?

Oh, there were a lot of interesting, attractive men and some exciting adventures, but no one seemed right until I met Neil. Suddenly it all seemed possible. It was the first time I had met an "appropriate man." Or so I thought...

PART VII

The Trip

CHAPTER NINETEEN

At times when it all seems right, the universe has a way of directing us, and now things all started to fall together.

Within twenty-four hours, Zane and I were on a plane to Los Angeles in pursuit of Neil and the Toyota. I sat there waiting for takeoff, not wanting to be there at all, but this time there was no place to run. I had to face it.

I said to Zane, "How about a drink?"

He said, "I think it's too early. I'll just have tomato juice." I ordered a Jack Daniels on the rocks.

He seemed extremely calm. Then he frowned and looked at me, "You know I really want to make this a quick trip. There's an earthquake predicted for Southern California which could be any day now." I smiled to myself about his worry over an earthquake! Somehow you never think much about them when you live in LA and it was the last thing that concerned me just then.

Fog covered Los Angeles as we landed – it seemed like a good omen. We headed for the car rental, and in no time we were driving up the coast toward Santa Monica. It felt strange not to be with Neil now. We had been back and forth to Los Angeles so many times together, picking each other up at airports or driving the truck back to Santa Fe with things from our houses in LA. Even now, when I arrived in an airport, I still got a twang of regret that he was no longer there to meet me.

Zane asked, "You sure you know where he lives?"

I nodded, "We stayed there just last year. He was sharing it with some film people to have a base in LA. Then he just sort of took it over when he moved back here. But I don't know if he's still living there."

Zane grimaced, "First we have to check that out."

"Yeah," I said. "He changed the phone number and made sure I never got the new one."

I didn't even know if he was still with his young girlfriend – the "grinning hyena" as I had labeled her. She had big Carol Channing eyes and a wide fixed smile and she certainly had hyena tendencies from the way she had pounced on Neil. The one time I saw her, I got the impression she was a few feet off the ground.

I had never met Neil's daughter – another of those voids in our relationship. But she was obviously his anima. He adored her and the "grinning hyena", who was only slightly older, certainly fit her pattern. He could relate to a daughter. In some ways he had been a father to me. He had bought me stuffed animals when I was sick (unlike my own father). This warm, caring side of him made it hard to believe he would lie to me.

Neil and my father were both kind, sweet men but remote in their own different ways. I thought of a dream Byron and I had analyzed:

I'm remodeling our summer house with my father. To my surprise, I look at the exterior and it's Victorian. My father waits in the truck while I go inside. I go down to the basement where I find a cult of people living. I try to tell them to keep it neat because the house is for sale and may be shown, but one woman talks very loudly not letting me be heard. I go upstairs and there's a young child in the kitchen, so I ask her to speak to them for me. The woman comes up and turns into an ugly, large insect right in front of our eyes. She starts eating the floor, then the leg of a chair. Slimy, little creatures get on my shoes.

Byron's comment: "Your Dad's not aware of any of this. He's out in the truck, so you have to deal with it alone."

I ask, "Why the Victorian facade? The actual house was a rambling, barn-like place with large beams and huge stone fireplaces." I had always loved this country house that my grandfather had built.

He says, "Victorian means old. Isn't that the old family? It's being chewed up by denial. Look at the woman – loud, self absorbed, evil, the devouring feminine. Were you devoured? Yep."

"What's the cult in the basement and why do I ask the child for help?"

"A cult is evil – banding together for no good. The levels of a house also represent levels of consciousness. Since you're in the basement, you're really in the unconscious. Also, an insect is pretty low on the evolutionary ladder – very primitive. You worry about being infected and ask the child to help. Isn't that you as a child? You can't confront the murderous cockroach head-on. And your father is out of touch in the truck. Neil's persona was that of the nurturing male, the open armed bear hug, everything safe in my arms…. But that was his mask. Underneath was the enraged child, dark basement time."

It was a grim one, but neither Neil nor my father knew how to relate or help me. Neil had feared closeness, spending many hours in front of the TV avoiding me. I thought of how I came to resent this and to hate the TV. Why did I put up with his distance? In the back of my mind something said: that's how it was at home. Wasn't it inevitable that a relationship became dull in time?

Byron was rambling on, "Neil tried to give people what they wanted, but there was a lot of rage underneath the role he played. No blame. The rage was because he was abandoned emotionally by his parents. That results in depression and anger."

I commented, "So it was really depression?"

"He stayed in the clouds because it was safer. He was a typical Flying Boy. Reality is too god-awful painful for them. They are cut off from their feelings. If you're not there, you don't get hurt."

This was disturbing and I still wasn't sure I could accept Byron's explanation. I said, "But in many ways he was sensitive and caring. He must have had some feelings?"

"Oh, I know, he appeared to be sensitive, acting as though he was in touch. He played a good part. But if Neil had stayed, it would have meant feeling and he couldn't do that. The nature of love is soaring, but groundedness is the only way to achieve real love. Real feeling and real caring are essential."

We met each other's needs. I, of course, helped him to "fly" by taking care of him and never making demands. He, in turn, played the role of the Ghostly Lover, a Jungian term for the idealized image of a lover. It makes mere mortals seem dull and ordinary, and I fell for it. He gave me the fantasy of having a loving relationship. But at the same time he was looking for *his* ideal in a woman, going from one to another – never finding the ideal. Obviously, it was all out of balance.

CHAPTER TWENTY

The building loomed up ahead in the mist rolling in from the ocean. It had been nearly deserted a year ago when we stayed there, but there was talk then of it being converted to condominiums.

I pointed out the apartment to Zane saying, "The place looks so different now. There were no security gates to the garage when we were here."

There was a light from a television in the apartment bedroom where we had stayed, but no one came into sight. We drove around and parked in a lot on the beach.

Zane said, "Wait here while I try to find a way into the building."

I had a long wait. There were a few people riding bicycles on the walk that led to Venice, and I watched the same Cadillac come into the parking lot and turn around about five times. It was eerie.

I thought of my childhood and that old summer home on the small lake in the mountains. It all seemed so safe. In contrast, the wild ocean always appeared gray and ominous. I thought of my little rowboat "Roxanne" that had been a childhood refuge.

The "Roxanne" was a gift from my parents one summer when I was about ten. I didn't have many clear memories of my early life, but I remembered being very excited and happy about the boat. I couldn't wait to try it out. My mother finally agreed to spend the night with me at the summer house, so I could go rowing the next morning.

The large old house was secluded at the foot of the mountain, and a caretaker named Mary lived year round above the garage. During the night, we thought we heard gunshots but were too terrified to look out the window. It was no dream. The next morning, Mary casually remarked that she had heard noises so she got out her shotgun. It was the last time we ever stayed there without my father. But it was one of the few fond memories I had of my mother.

The "Roxanne" became my escape. I would take pillows, books and a big hat with me to sit out there on the lake among the frogs and turtles where it was quiet, away from all my mother's turmoil. I listened to the crickets and read for hours, looking for answers in the classics. Shakespeare became too tedious. Then I discovered Tennessee Williams. In a strange way, I found comfort in reading his plays. I could identify with them for some bizarre reason. They made it seem all right to have a crazy, distant family. In comparison to his characters, my family seemed almost normal or at least interesting.

By then I was in college living in a world of ideas, thinking I had found the answer. What sort of person was I in those days? I doubted that I was in touch with my feelings. I couldn't remember what I looked like or how I dressed, except for a black turtle-neck sweater and a favorite raincoat. I went to classes and played in the college orchestra, living in my head more than my body. Yet it was still difficult going home, and I went armed with books to escape my family.

As I went back in time, I tried to think of my mother. I regretted that I had never been close to her. Too bad I hadn't known her as a person and not as my mother. Other people saw her vivacious, entertaining persona, not the depressed and angry shadow side behind the facade. Inside I think she was way ahead of her time – a talented woman who found no place to be in her era. Not many women had careers or had the courage to get divorced in her day.

I was beginning to recognize that she gave me a lot – teaching me music and taking me to every concert that came to the area. It was important to her that I learn the cello. As far as school was concerned, teaching me to cook or things mothers ordinarily taught daughters, it didn't interest her. So it wasn't important.

I thought of when Marion Anderson came to sing at a nearby college — I was quite young. There wasn't a good hotel in town and Mom wanted to invite her to stay with us. But my father said "no". That was when I first saw the prejudice in our town and realized my mother didn't feel that way. She was different, in a good way!

*   *   *

My thoughts came back to the present as I saw Zane appear through the fog – on foot. I watched him come toward me. He wasn't tall, but he had an engaging smile and was at ease in the world. Here I sat dressed for the caper in a black shirt and sneakers with my rain hat pulled down over my eyes hiding in the car. Zane was wearing shorts, a white shirt, and tennis shoes – more the All American Boy look than that of a car thief. I was so glad he had come with me. I still didn't want to deal with the search and here he was enjoying the whole adventure. I was with the right friend at the right time!

It took real guts to be a thief, even if you were stealing your own truck. I reminded myself it was legal to steal your own truck.

I reached over to open the door, "Zane, I was getting worried. Did you find it?"

He looked calm but puzzled, "No. I got past security and into the building. There are two levels of parking and I went through it all, but there wasn't a Toyota truck." He never explained how he got in, but it didn't matter.

I looked at my watch. It was nearly 10:00 P.M. I said, "Let's go have some dinner. I remember a nice little restaurant in Venice."

We drove down the coast. The main street looked different than I remembered and the restaurant was no longer there. We spotted a little Italian place with an outside courtyard which was nearly empty, but the smell of the pizza drew us in. We sat outside in the damp night air. I ordered pasta and wine which wasn't great, but I managed to eat something and felt a little better.

I asked Zane, "So what do you think we should do next?"

He looked a bit discouraged, "We may as well go back and see if he's turned up, but for some reason I doubt it. Let's have some coffee, kill a little more time before we go."

I couldn't think of any wonderful ideas and the whole saga seemed to fall a bit flat. Maybe Neil had moved; then how would we find him? We finished the coffee and headed back to the building.

There was a parking space right in front where we could look up at the apartment window. Zane checked out the garage again, but found no truck. By midnight it seemed unlikely that Neil would appear.

I yawned, saying, "Let's go to my friend's house and get some sleep. Maybe tomorrow things will look brighter." He agreed, so we headed toward Hollywood, feeling a bit disillusioned.

My friend, Rachael, had left me a key to her house as she was away. We were exhausted and baffled by the time we arrived there, but her cat gave us a loud welcome, glad that we had come to keep her company.

I thought of one more possibility and said to Zane, "There's something we ought to check out. I called Neil at an office number months ago and I think I remember the name of the company. Something like The Sound Studio.

I'll see if it's listed in the telephone book before we go to bed."

I was afraid it was just one more recording studio at MGM or Warner Brothers with guards at the gates. There was nothing in the Hollywood directory. But we were in luck! There it was listed in the West LA phone book in what sounded like an office building.

I fell into bed full of renewed hope with Tiger Lilly happily purring at my side. She reminded me of Siegfried.

Neil had left Siegfried behind with the rest of his belongings. But poor Siegfried didn't survive very long. I took him to the vet one day and after many tests I was told he had kitty leukemia. I tried everything the vet suggested. A few months later, Siegfried was too sick to go on. Perhaps he missed Neil. I said goodbye to him, telling him if he wanted to reincarnate he was welcome to come back.

Well, to my surprise, a lovely grey cat arrived at my bedroom window about six months later. He wanted to come in and wouldn't take no for an answer. Bootsie hissed and screamed at him; Sage got all furry with a gigantic tail. I let him in eventually after locking my two cats out of the room. I picked him up and his long body lay in my arms and he just purred and purred.

I knew it was Siegfried, because he had climbed the screens as a kitten until Neil had taken him in. Of course, he never left. One of the things I loved about Neil was his compassion for animals. This time I knew I couldn't keep Siegfried – my cats were too upset. I found him a good home and let him go, in spite of my guilt and sadness.

I'd always adored cats. They look you straight in the eye when you talk to them.

CHAPTER TWENTY-ONE

Later, Byron called it an "adventure in rebalancing". He was very proud that I had taken action and was no longer playing the victim, taking care of people. It had been a Catch 22 situation. I loved Neil and when disaster struck, as it often did, I was always there to take care of the situation. Then he resented it and blamed me for wanting control.

Byron said, "Control is always fear based."

"But," I tried to explain to Byron, "we were 'together'. I couldn't desert him and say 'you take care of your own problems, don't look at me!' I thought it was a lasting kind of relationship. Oh, there were things to resolve, but I thought I was capable of dealing with it."

"Alas!" he exclaimed, "that immediately put you into the role of his mother."

That shut me up and made me think. It placed me "in control", I realized, so I became the ogre. Had I been weak, helpless and sympathetic (like the blonde), I would have been more lovable, I guess, but then what a mess our lives would have been.

Byron asked me to relate the dream I had the night before. It was about a war with the Indians:

There's a tall man who I think is Neil, but doesn't look like him. He comes out of a hospital and I tell him his car has been demolished in a war with the Indians. It's a wreck in front of the hospital – you can't even tell it's a car. I'm looking at a large box of furry Eskimo puppies on the street that belong to the Indians.

"Byron, I don't know what to make of this one."

"I do," he grinned smugly, "The vehicle is your old animus being dismantled, thank God. I like it. Cars get demolished when they are off course." Was that why Neil had the wreck soon after leaving me? I wondered. "The hospital is a place of healing, ha, ha. The Indians represent the shadow and the war's with them!"

"Oh, that's good, isn't it?"

"I think they represent your positive emerging animus in this case. It could also be native wisdom, so the Indians are the good guys here. They are wrecking the car and they also own the puppies."

"In the dream, I'm trying to figure out if the puppies in the box are dead or alive. Obviously those are my feelings."

"Yes, the animals represent feelings and that's a hell of a box of feelings you're sorting out. The puppies belong to the Indians. They're feelings left from the conflict. The old animus is finally burned out. You don't need it anymore. Once you were infected with it."

"OK, so why am I afraid to look at anyone again, to be involved? I never went through this before."

"Many times burned, twice shy. Because now you're more conscious, my dear, not as unconscious – that's when you replicate the same pattern until you get it. I think that's what I attribute the tears and frustration to. I like it. I don't have a problem with any of it. You don't have to be his mother anymore, but you're still looking at the feelings."

As usual he revealed stuff I hadn't seen in the dream and I felt better with the understanding that came out of his analysis.

My work with Byron involving the struggle to change my animus, or prototype of the male I chose to love, was finally showing progress. I had been attracted to the old sick, weak animus for a long time but recent dreams were beginning to show change.

* * *

I awoke to the "adventure" with the sound of the sprinkler system at 6:00 A.M. Rachael's bedroom was a large, sunny room with a window overlooking the city and I didn't want to move. I could hear Zane already in the shower as I went downstairs to make coffee. I knew he would be anxious to get going.

As he sipped coffee, Zane said, "Let's get out of here and have breakfast later."

I took my coffee along in an effort to keep my eyes open. As we got into the car, I asked, "Where to first? Do you think he still lives in that apartment?"

Zane mumbled, "I kind of doubt it, but we've got to check it out."

It was a long drive out to the ocean and we didn't feel much like talking. By 7:00 A.M. we boldly sat in front of the apartment building. I saw a light go off in the living room of the apartment, but no truck appeared. I felt sure they had moved somewhere else at this point. Cars zoomed out of the garage – the whole world was going to work.

Then a white car went by with a man and a woman in it and I yelled, "It's Neil. I only had a fast glimpse, but it was his profile."

We raced down the Pacific Coast Highway after them. Catching a glimpse of them as we drew near, Neil said, "I think it *is* Neil."

We raced through Venice and into Marina del Rey where the white car stopped by a coffee shop. When a middle aged waitress stepped from the car, we realized the man wasn't Neil. We agreed he did have a similar profile. Dejected we went into the restaurant to have a doughnut and bad coffee.

It was still only about eight in the morning so we plotted what to do until we could call The Sound Studio at nine. Zane said, "I think I'll call Sarah in Santa Fe. She may have kept in touch with Neil and might have a telephone number." It sounded plausible because I had a feeling she was an old girlfriend of his.

Zane found a telephone and dialed her number, making up an excuse to get Neil's telephone number. He said he wanted to return some books to Neil before he left for

Fredericka Heller

Mexico in a few days. But she wasn't about to give out a home number or address. Another defeat.

By now it was nearly nine. There was the one chance that Neil was still working at The Sound Studio – our last chance.

When Zane dialed the number, I couldn't believe it – Neil was there. They had a friendly chat about the books and Zane's trip to Mexico, and then Neil had to take another call. He said he'd call Zane back. We had all we needed.

As we drove up the Coast Highway, I remembered my dream that night at Rachael's house:

I'm involved in a war and they tell us it's time to go fight. But we can't find any guns and have nothing to fight with. Then I find a pistol, but I don't know how to use it. They never taught the women how to shoot, so there's not much we can do in the war.

CHAPTER TWENTY-TWO

I cringed at the thought of the next move. Thank God Zane had the mentality of a good spy. For all I knew maybe he was in the CIA and this was just a diversion for him. There were a number of CIA agents living around Santa Fe. I didn't really know Zane very well or even why he was helping me, but I intuitively trusted him as a friend. It was the synchronicity of timing that made it feel right.

I thought of a dream I had discussed with Byron not too long ago. For months I didn't want to face what was happening or deal with any of it. But the promise of change had shown up in a dream.

Gardeners are cleaning up my garden early in the morning before dawn. A friend comes by and I'm distracted. I look out to see the gardeners removing all of my aspen trees and taking them away. I run after them to retrieve the trees, but they have gone.

Byron asked, "What do gardeners do?"

I thought for a moment, then answered, "Well, they clean up the garden, plant flowers…

Byron cut in, "Yes, they clean out stuff that's not needed. And what about aspens?"

The fall aspens came to mind. Every October there were groves of brilliant yellow aspens on the mountain slopes on the way to the ski area. "They're beautiful in the fall when the leaves turn. And there's something delicate and fragile about them when they sway in the wind."

Byron nodded, "Yeah, and they grow in groves, one root system, not deeply rooted either. They stand together and die together, very vulnerable, not like a sturdy oak." He paused, then his face lit up, "And you're right, there is something delicate and fragile about them and I think it's clearing out the fragility in you, making way for new growth."

I asked, "Why does the friend come by and distract me?"

"I think she's a part of your psyche trying to clean up the unconscious. This takes place in a time of darkness before the dawn, when you can't see things very clearly.

She distracts you so the gardeners can get the fragile aspens out and then help clean up the unconscious to make room for your individuation."

I was finally doing it, getting ready for a new future and resolving the past – making room for new growth!

* * *

We pulled up in front of the building in West LA and drove into a small garage with very few cars. A sign said it was for the Animal Rescue League. There was another large parking garage in back. Zane asked the attendant for rates saying he might be working in the building soon. We parked and he went to explore the second floor. What if he ran into Neil? Worse yet, what if I saw him? The anxiety sharply increased. I saw Zane returning. He looked grim as he bluntly stated, "Nothing." We drove out and into a lot across the street – no red truck. Then I saw another entrance to the building on the side. Zane parked on the street and walked up the ramp past the attendant.

There were about a dozen Mexicans standing around on the street. I suppose they were waiting for people to hire them for the day. Maybe we were near an unemployment office. I guess it was a slow day for them and they all seemed to be watching us.

Time dragged as I waited. My mind wandered back to Neil, still caught in the web of trying to comprehend our past.

A month after our breakup, I had gone to see an astrologer/numerologist. When I first got together with Neil, it had seemed so right. I think we really loved each other. I wanted to know what was in the cosmos that had caused it all to fall apart so disastrously. Byron had said Neil was attracted to me as it was a chance to get his life on a stable path. It was a promise of solidity, safety, sanity for him. And I thought I was finding all of that in Neil. We were both ready for a solid, sane relationship. As Byron put it, "You were both in the same place at the same time. You don't attract a person who isn't of the same mind set, whether neurotic, sane, or crazy." So why hadn't it worked?

Tamara, the numerologist, was an earthy-looking, strong woman who rambled on at a fast pace. Everything she said seemed to be something I should hang onto and take seriously. She had brought up an interesting aspect of my relationship with Neil. Seven was my karmic number which represented an area I had to work out in this lifetime, having to do with finding faith in myself and the universe. I thought of how I had stayed in the background with Neil. Now I began to understood why.

I never had to compete. I had no sisters or brothers so I never learned to compete. Did I need to learn to be competitive now? I never even competed against other women, figuring men either liked me for my qualities or they didn't.

No, that wasn't it. Suddenly, it struck me – I could never compete with Neil or other women because it would be like competing with my mother!

It seems that the years I spent with Neil were "seven" years. I'm sure that meant that I had a lot of karma to work out with him but, obviously, I wasn't very successful at resolving it. Tamara explained that now I was finally coming out of the "sevens" and getting into an "eight" era, which had more to do with getting a place of power and authority.

She smiled as she said, "You need to stand up and say: 'this is what I want to do'. Not aggressively, but managing to fill the mold you've earned." (I remembered the dream about the turtle that Byron had interpreted as revealing my fear of power.)

"After all," she continued, "it's time we realized that humility is a spiritual error." I thought about that one a lot.

This sounded challenging and exciting. I felt there was a ring of truth to all of it. She said I still had to solve power and authority issues with men. I certainly hadn't dealt much with this issue with Neil. I had constantly come to his rescue and bailed him out – financially as well as every other way. But I hadn't stood up to him as an equal. I hadn't made demands. I didn't know it was a game that I had to win or a competition.

The synchronicity of events is amazing. I looked at an astrology book when I got home and found an apt description of Neil. I should have read about his sign before getting involved. It said:

> "Mates of this sign are somewhat hard to handle in the sense that it is often difficult to get a grip on what they really want from you. They may wear their superficial emotions on their faces, but keep their real feelings closely behind a mask. Many a client with a mate in this sign has consulted an astrologer and said, "I thought everything was fine. Then he just walked out!"

* * *

Well, I never thought everything was fine during the last year we were together, but with Byron's help I was sure we could work it out. I hadn't realized that Neil didn't want to – that was hidden by his mask.

CHAPTER TWENTY-THRE

Then I saw Zane appear – all smiles. He leaned on the window and said, "I've found the truck! The bad news is, the key doesn't work." My heart sank. Now I knew we'd never get it.

But, undaunted, we went in search of a locksmith finding one a few blocks away. Zane went in and I heard him saying, "We're locked out of our car..." Then he gave the locksmith the code we had, only to find there was supposed to be a letter that went with the code. I hoped we wouldn't need to try all 26 letters in the alphabet to get the right combination.

Finally the locksmith made another key for us and I drove back to the building, dropping Zane at the front this time, then parking by the exit. The Mexicans were all watching. I put my hat on as I slid down in the seat.

Thoughts of Neil were so vivid now that I was back in Los Angeles. We had been here just a few months before the breakup. He was still moving things out to Santa Fe which I thought he considered home, so I didn't have a clue that he was thinking of leaving. Maybe he wasn't intending to leave at that point. Maybe it was a spur of the moment decision after he met the blonde.

He had given up his rental house in LA, and we loaded the truck with tropical plants that he had left in the garden when he sublet the house. As usual, we were late leaving and by evening ran into a terrible snow storm an hour outside of Flagstaff, even though it was March. The poor plants sat in the freezing weather all night. I still have some of those plants, still trying to doctor them back to life.

Rescuing had become an obsession. I probably would never have given up on our relationship. I always had to make things work. I always had to finish a painting, no matter how long it took to rework it.

I thought of the paintings I had done in the years I was with Neil. My work had changed. The colors were more intense and heavier. These were large abstract paintings with looming, giant shadow forms. I hadn't realized this before. The shapes had just appeared from my sub-conscious. In one painting, there were two ominous figures on each side and a small dove escaping out the top. Another, one of my most recent paintings, had two heart shapes slipping down the canvas and off the bottom.

In the beginning I'd had a lot of illusions about the relationship. I thought it would solve everything. I always searched for that certain peace of mind that creative work demands. Some balance in my life seemed necessary so that I didn't feel lonely and could focus on my work. However, I never really attained that kind of security with Neil. Instead there were too many distractions and my work suffered as a result of being with him.

Painting was always a struggle, but a rewarding struggle when I completed a new canvas and it all suddenly fell together. I'd feel elated about it, a real high. But then there were times when it wasn't going well, when I'd feel down and depressed. At those times I knew I couldn't paint. I was fooling myself to even think that I was an artist. Then, picking up a brush was a real struggle. I always thought: "If only I had a close relationship – that would be the answer because I wouldn't feel insecure working alone in my studio." Now I know it doesn't work that way.

In my efforts to unravel the whole mess, trying to understand love, I read an interesting book by Dr. Harville Hendrix called *Getting the Love You Want*. In this book Dr. Hendrix zeroed right in on the whole thing, but stating it from a different point of view from Jung. Yet he arrived at much the same conclusions.

Whereas, in Jungian therapy, we worked to change the animus from a dark, destructive one, developed in childhood by our role models, to one that is harmonious and loving, Harville Hendrix describes much the same thing calling it the Old Brain.

He says we underestimate the unconscious mind. He explains that the Old Brain selects the ones we're attracted to as mates by picking ones like our parents, who have the same negative traits. Apparently we do this subconsciously, so we can finally work out the problems we had as children and get what we needed from our parents.

But there's a hitch. He explains how we fall into the same trap because we run into the same problems we had in relating to the parents. We not only have to ask for what we want of the relationship, but we must make changes in our own responses. Yet he gives us some good advice on how to communicate, pointing out that you can only change yourself. By taking a new role you get a new response. I wish I had read this while I was still with Neil.

It was another, clearer interpretation of why I kept falling for the same dark, shadow "types" over and over, though they appeared to have different exteriors. I was beginning to understand it. Neil hadn't been different at all – just his exterior seemed more acceptable. He fell into the same old pattern: self-absorbed and distant. For me it was no more possible to have a close relationship with him, than it had been with my parents.

PART VIII

Recovery

CHAPTER TWENTY-FOUR

When Neil left I was angry – at the deception, at the betrayal, the lies, the lost illusions, all of it. Being angry made me feel like my mother, so I fought it. I was still trying not to be like my mother! All my life I tried not to be like my mother.

Recently I had an amazing session with yet another astrologer in Santa Fe. It was uncanny how she described my family.

"Your mother was very skitzy – lots of anger, almost violent. She was explosive."

I asked, "Can you see that in *my* chart?"

She nodded, "Oh, yes, you were frightened. How do you deal with an explosive, unpredictable mother? She was supposed to love and nurture you, but she couldn't even do that for herself. You became the caretaker at a very early age. So, it's almost as if now the test is to move yourself into a situation or role where there is a balance, where you get nurtured and cared for. When you've been strong and had to cope all your life, this is the hard part. Emotions had to be put on the back burner, because you were dealing with survival."

"How do you see my father?"

"Your father had to live with a crazy woman, so what he did was detach. Did he stay married to her?"

"Yes.

"Wow, he was like the martyr."

"We both detached."

She went on, "Yeah, so you've always been somewhat detached, in a sense, from life. The big thing, when a child is raised with a parent who is disturbed, is safety. We never feel safe. There's always the element of what's going to happen next."

It was what Byron had read in my dreams all along.

* * *

Byron told me to look at the anger and it was disturbing when I realized I was angry inside, not just angry at Neil. He told me to be good to "me" (that Inner Child that I now recognized as so important).

When I was a child I saw a movie that haunted me for years. All I could remember was a little girl playing on a big grassy lawn. Then she went into a large house and never came out again. I identified with that little girl and wondered what happened to her. I was too young to understand the movie, but years later I discovered it was *King's Row,* when I saw it on late night TV.

I don't know how I happened to see that movie as a child. I was probably allowed to go to a Saturday matinee, so that I could follow the next episode of "Superman," a series which had been running for years.

To my surprise, when I saw *King's Row* on television it was in black and white and I had vividly remembered green grass. The rest of the movie I had forgotten, but I have never liked green grass. Perhaps that was part of what attracted me to the desert when I moved to Santa Fe.

King's Row was about a young girl who is killed by her father when he realizes she has inherited her mother's insanity. He then commits suicide. I guess it was a bit complex for a child to comprehend, so it got stuck somewhere in the subconscious for all those years.

Nevertheless, my "child" had retreated and not come out again for many years. Now I was trying to be nice to that child and find her again – listening to what she wanted, trying to get her to emerge and trying to understand who she was. It seemed to be working! Somehow I felt much better. I took trips, I bought myself clothes, I didn't force myself to do anything. I even stopped painting for a time! I had been disciplining myself, making *me* paint as my mother had made me practice the cello.

And it helped me to get over the affair. Otherwise, I could never be doing this – chasing after a truck! Yet now I was feeling guilty. This was totally out of character for me. My role had been to take care of Neil. At the same time, I was proud of myself for doing it. "It", retrieving the truck, had something to do with regaining my self-esteem – looking out for myself.

* * *

Suddenly Zane jumped into the car interrupting my reminiscing. "I think we better look for another locksmith – this key doesn't work." Even Zane seemed a bit anxious at this point. We drove around until we found another locksmith shop.

The irony of it suddenly occurred me. Here we were trying to find the right key, and I was trying to find the key to comprehending my self! I laughed at myself as I recognized this obsession with keys.

I went into the shop with Zane. We explained our dilemma and the locksmith looked at us actually scratching his head. Then his face lit up and he said, "I know an old man – you gotta go about five miles down the freeway, then turn off at exit 218." He paused. "Can't remember the guy's name, but he's just up the hill to the left. If anyone could figure it out, he could."

We thanked him and hurriedly returned to the car. We raced down the freeway not daring to hope. I said, "Look, that's the exit! Then we turn left up that hill!" We finally found the place just before noon and it occurred to me that Neil might be going to lunch – in the truck. The old man took ages pondering over the code books and looking at keys. I was getting impatient. Then finally we had another key, and we dashed back to the office building.

CHAPTER TWENTY-FIVE

I nervously waited in the car as Zane once again went past the guard into the parking lot. I didn't feel too hopeful. It seemed like an eternity before I saw the red truck appear. We had done it! I felt limp. Now I couldn't believe we had done it! I felt awful.

Byron later explained, "When you recaptured the truck, you recognized the finality of love lost. There was no turning back. There could no longer be any hope of reconciliation. It's the last act that brings lots of mourning and grief and finality. But there's also the redemption side of establishing boundaries, of not being a victim – the clarity of redemption of self, as we face the loss of love."

Zane shouted that I should follow him to the locksmith to thank the old man and get more keys made. When I met him there, he was laughing as he told me about it, "I just waved at the parking attendant as I drove out, and he waved back."

Zane followed me back to Rachael's house through half of LA with numerous detours. I was definitely feeling guilty about the truck now. I also felt sad.

I realized that I could have played the role, denied that anything was wrong, and perhaps still be with Neil. But it would have been exhausting and degrading. It had a lot to do with why I never married. I couldn't keep feelings and thoughts to myself. They needed to be expressed, preferably to someone close to me. I needed to relate! I also needed to know what was going on in a man's head or there would be a big gulf between us. I kept running into big gulfs!

But there had been a lot of breakups among our friends in the last few years – not just us. Who wants a destructive relationship? If there's no balance or communication, it can't ever work. It's no longer "anything to make it *work*". I thought of the words to an old song by Melanie in the Seventies: "I'm sorry I saw you. I meant to stay blind".

When I looked at my parents, there had been little communication. As a kid, I knew there had to be more to life somewhere out there and I was going to find it. I thought it was just my family, but I think it was a whole generation. We learned to conform. It also explained why everyone seemed to be from a "dysfunctional family". I had looked for something real, but it had been a long search.

I remembered a conversation with Sam about his dysfunctional family. He came from a family of alcoholics. He was angry, blaming them for his problems all of his life. I didn't want to do that. I thought, in contrast, the most pleasant times I had with my family were evenings when we had a few drinks. It was about the only time there was any conversation and laughter. I guess I was lucky. At least my parents weren't alcoholics!

*   *   *

Byron had suggested I look at my mother's side of the family to have some understanding of her childhood. My mother had grown up in a family of musicians in Wales. I distinctly remember the movie "Five Easy Pieces," which really struck home. I came out of the theater in a dreadful state of depression, whereas my friends saw it as just another entertaining movie. The film was about a family of musicians. Achievement was valued over any caring or love among the family members, and to me it was about the alienation the family suffered.

It was important to my mother that I become a good musician and I understood her ingrained attitude after seeing that movie. It came from her background.

In order to learn more about my mother's childhood, I spoke to my English aunt who had been married to her brother. She was very proper and opinionated, but quite willing to tell me all she knew about my mother. It wasn't much. But it became apparent that my mother had been through several very traumatic incidents. Her mother, a Victorian, had run a hotel in Wales after my grandfather, who was diabetic, overdosed in a pastry shop when he was in his thirties. They never discussed whether or not he'd committed suicide but I think, understandably, my grandmother was quite angry and disturbed over it. His death must have had an effect on my mother, who was only about eleven at the time, but she never mentioned the incident or her feelings about her father.

Then my mother's brother contracted TB in his teens and was sent to live on an orange plantation in Kenya, where the climate was dryer. (He later came to the States, eventually becoming very successful in frozen orange juice.)

But my mother grew up in the Queens Hotel and apparently had very little family life. She became stage struck by the traveling theatrical groups who stayed at the hotel. When she was about twenty, she won a voice competition that brought her to New York. While searching through old albums, I found some wonderful photos of her on stage at the Roxy Theater, and others of her singing in nightclubs.

I began to realize that I came from a family of strong women, but God forbid that I became strong and competed with them! This brought back those childhood insecurities and I began to shrink. My mother was so critical! I never seemed to please her but then I didn't know she was unconventional. I thought that was normal behavior. As Byron said: "We were wired backwards as children!"

Yet, I could see more and more how my mother influenced me in a positive way to become an artist. I never wanted to go on with music, but painting became my obsession. She had a difficult, neurotic life, but she gave me an important gift – that of creativity and a love of the arts.

*   *   *

When I thought of the last half of my mother's life, I felt as Gloria Steinem did when she stated in her book that she cried over my mother's life, not her death. I felt compassion for her, if not closeness.

The night my mother died, I was in California. I thought I was getting the flu and went to bed early. I was freezing cold, but when I awoke about six in the morning I felt just fine. Then, a disturbing thought struck me – my mother died and maybe she had been trying to reach me. Her death wasn't unexpected as she had been ill for a long time. About seven o'clock the phone rang confirming my fears.

I dutifully flew home for the funeral. My Welsh uncle arrived the following day. No one seemed very emotional about it, except maybe the neighbors. Actually it was a relief. But the neighbors would come to the door with grim expressions bringing a stew or a pie, asking how my father was doing. I couldn't very well say he was next door in the cemetery hitting golf balls, so I made up something, not being familiar with funeral protocol.

I stood uncomfortably between my father and my uncle at the funeral, as the minister pontificated about my exceptional mother. My uncle quietly mumbled to me, "How long does this go on?"

I replied, "I have no idea. I've never been to one before."

On the way out, he turned to me in an exasperated voice and said, "When I go, no one is going through this sort of thing. I'm being cremated."

Then we went to my father's house for some good strong drinks. It turned into a party my mother would have loved.

CHAPTER TWENTY-SIX

As I drove into Rachael's driveway, I saw Zane not far behind in the truck. I waited for him and he smiled as he got out, saying, "Let's get packed. I'm ready to get out of here."

In no time we packed and threw everything in the back of the truck. If Neil had any suspicions about my involvement in the disappearance of the truck, this would be the first place he would look. We had stayed with Rachael many times.

She was a screenwriter who was very much a part of the Hollywood scene. But being a writer, she also lived in her own little world and garden. She had a very green thumb and a very perceptive mind. I think I related to one part of her world, but no one related to all of it.

I looked at Rachael's garden where I had spent many wonderful hours by the pool. The numerous varieties of tropical plants had been the inspiration for some of my paintings. After the darkness of the New York art world, my move to Los Angeles was a startling contrast. It was here that I found a direction for my painting in the colorful, lush plants of the Southwest. I knew that was the reason for my move. In the California sunlight I began to realize I could no longer paint the dark, heavy abstractions I had painted in New York. The transition started when I noticed the brilliant light on the banana leaves and palm fronds. I may also have been influenced psychologically by an environment that took little seriously, where I felt lighter.

I remember the dark struggle of the New York art world in the late fifties and sixties; the search for new directions. It had a strong effect on me as an art student at a time when everyone drank heavily, escaping in alcohol from the problems of trying to survive as an artist in a tough city. We would go to the Cedar Bar after class and talk about painting with other artists. I was young and always on the edge, yet extremely influenced by the heavy depressive mood, the seriousness and idealism of that period.

Los Angeles was a different world. When someone asked me if I had fun painting, it felt trivial like a sharp insult. Painting was something I took seriously and I wasn't sure I would like the art scene in LA.

*   *   *

I heard Zane calling me from the kitchen door. "Don't you think we should call Beth at the bank before we leave? We ought to tell her we've got the truck."

I went into the kitchen and got her on the phone. She sounded amazed. She said they had all been rooting for us. They couldn't believe we found the truck so fast.

The timing had been perfect. She explained, "Neil called just this morning when he got the bank's letter of intent to repossess the truck. He said he had sent a check and couldn't imagine what happened to it. I reminded him that he now owed two months' payments and he didn't seem very happy about that. Oh, and when I asked him where the truck was, he lied! He said it was in Santa Fe. Can you imagine, he lied!"

The realization hit me as I replied, "Of course, the original letter was sent to Santa Fe P.O. Box. He never got it." When Beth found his current address, an LA P.O. Box, she sent it out to him immediately.

She advised us to get out of California as fast as possible and back to New Mexico, where the truck was registered. She said, "I won't take the call if he tries to reach me this afternoon." I looked at Zane as I hung up.

Zane said, "OK, we've done it. Let's go."

He followed me down La Cienega to return the rental car to Hertz, which was out by the airport. Every time I looked back, I felt as though Neil was in that truck – ghosts of the past. Feelings of anger and frustration returned as I thought of him. He had been so charming, so charismatic, but so doomed to failure. It was very sad and yet I knew now he wouldn't/couldn't change. I think the sadness was more about what could have been, not what was.

CHAPTER TWENTY-SEVEN

I continued to reflect on the affair. The end had occurred exactly four years from the start of the affair – appropriately enough on the Fourth of July weekend, the celebration of the Declaration of Independence. Now I realized that was why July 4th had always been significant in my life. (To quote Byron: "Looking for the Self is looking for Independence Day!") Now it all seemed to make more sense, as the pieces were fitting together like the last part of a puzzle.

Santa Fe is probably the only place where the Fourth of July weekend is celebrated by the opening of the opera. The setting is out in the hills with views of the Sangre de Cristo Mountains behind the Opera House and the Jemez

Mountains in back of the stage. There are usually spectacular sunsets just before curtain.

My last "date" with Neil was opening night at the opera. We had driven out with friends for the traditional tailgate party in the parking lot of the opera house that evening. Everyone was dressed in exotic formal attire. Some of the parties were very elaborate, catered affairs with tables and chairs, and others were simply held on tailgates or on the bed of trucks. As we were getting hor d'oeuvres and wine out of the picnic basket, it started to rain. Everyone rushed for cover.

Rather than wait we decided to eat in the car. The rain was heavy, the sky looked dense and Neil was unusually quiet. It became humid and heavy in the car. I was feeling extremely uncomfortable and our friends became distressed by the atmosphere. The weather cleared up just in time for the champagne reception before the opera and we gladly escaped from the car, but I had a strange sense of doom the whole evening.

The opera was spectacular and the stars slowly emerged from behind the clouds as we watched the lightning in the distance. There was a certain magic about the music in the open theater. I had become an avid opera lover after moving to Santa Fe and Neil's mood was not going to ruin the evening for me.

* * *

It was the following night that I tried to call Neil at the studio where he was working on some new electronic music. A bad thunderstorm had come up suddenly causing the lights to go out. I looked at the sky, which had turned a midnight blue. There were explosions of white light against the blue sky, like bombs going off over the hill. It was frightening, and I didn't like being alone. The flashes of lightning leaped across the sky, horizontal at times.

I knew Neil would have to turn off the computer in the storm. When I got the answering machine, I instinctively knew he wasn't there. I sat on the bed in the dark staring out at the night. Then the rain started pelting the skylights and running down the windows. It was noisy and turbulent. You could barely hear the thunder. My head seemed to be in the same kind of turmoil.

I couldn't suppress the anger and frustration anymore, but at the same time I didn't want to face him. The night dragged on endlessly. I couldn't concentrate on anything. I was in the jacuzzi tub trying to calm down when he got home about midnight. The bubbling water seemed comforting. Neil walked in all smiles and I asked, "Where have you been? I've been trying to call you all evening."

He thought nothing of lying and said, "I've been working. Oh, I guess the phone was turned off." I glared at him. I think he realized that I knew and I wouldn't take it anymore.

We got into bed and held hands. I said, "Neil, this can't ever work if I can't trust you." He didn't respond.

* * *

He left the next morning and came back for his clothes that night, leaving everything else behind. I eventually put most of his possessions in a storage unit.

I didn't know where he had gone. Then I heard he was staying in a friend's guest house, so I called Gailey a week later to ask how he was.

In her outspoken way, she said, "My dear, he's madly in love. He brought her to dinner, an attractive young blonde – we expected you to be with him and didn't know what to say. They held hands all night!"

I was in shock. Then she told me about the others – the Australian acupuncturist, Edie, who vowed he was the man she intended to spend the rest of her life with. Gailey went on, as though she finally had to tell me all of it, "Edie was terribly upset when she learned that he was also having an affair with the secretary at the film company. But this little blonde one will be a real shock, when she returns from Europe and hears about her!"

I said, "Christ, what a bastard!" Then I slammed down the phone.

At some point, I started to look at it realistically. I had fallen into a seductive trap – taking care of this man, thinking I needed him. I suppose it could be called "co-dependence" in analytical terms.

I knew what had happened. I had become overly responsible to compensate for Neil's lack of responsibility. It was my fault that I had accepted this role without complaint. I was much too passive. I kept my feelings to myself, afraid to confront Neil, afraid he would leave. I tried ridiculously hard to please him and it had worked for awhile.

I never got angry or questioned him. He didn't want to be questioned, but then I saw I was only encouraging his secretiveness. I was playing his game! He kept a lot of stuff to himself, so it became harder and harder to get through those barriers. He had become estranged and remote. The magic had gone with everything else. Why the hell had I put up with it for so long?

Now I realized how we both contributed to the lack of communication. But the big difference, I think, was that he was protecting himself, while I was trying to make it work for us.

I guess it had disintegrated into one of those relationships where he expected me to take care of him and have no demands or expectations, as long as he stayed around. When we made love there was no passion. Maybe it had all become too routine for him. He was addictive, needed the excitement of something new. He wanted sensation, not love. I couldn't reach him on any level and yet something, somewhere deep inside me, had expected a miraculous breakthrough that never came.

I had dreams about big clouds forming over my pool and then there would be crashing waves.

PART IX

Return to the Desert

CHAPTER TWENTY-EIGHT

After Zane and I returned the rental car, we set off toward the desert through thick smog, past burned-out parts of LA from the riots years ago. The city went on endlessly. It was so good to be on our way. I glanced around the inside of the truck. There was a steering-wheel lock. I looked at Zane and he commented, "Yeah, he would have put it on this afternoon when he got the repossession letter!

I said, "We did it just in time. Why do I feel so bad leaving him without a truck?" I looked at Neil's hat and some cushions that made me feel uncomfortable.

Zane laughed again, at me this time. Shaking his head he said, "You still don't get it, do you? He didn't care about you. He was using you, and he wouldn't think twice about taking the truck back if he could, so we've got to be careful." Zane had grown up in Texas and had that direct way of speaking with a slight drawl that made his outspoken criticism sound OK.

The "recovery" had taken us less than twenty-four hours and I was more than ready to get out of the city. LA had come to represent materialism, power games, all that I had wanted to leave behind when I moved to Santa Fe. It now seemed like a dark, unconscious, underground place. I realized Neil was too caught up in all of it to ever leave. He loved the game.

There was an article in *The New Mexican*, the Santa Fe newspaper, by Larry Brody, a Hollywood writer and producer, about why he had moved to Santa Fe. At first he couldn't quite explain why he had left LA. Then he began to realize the oppression he had felt there: "You are made to feel you have no worth as a human being unless you happen to be rich." He went on to say, "I don't mean well-to-do. Or even wealthy. I mean really, really rich – Rolls Royce rich. (I thought of poor Ramon.) Malibu Beach house rich. Especially if you're in show business where image is everything. And image costs money. The cars, the clothes, the houses...."

I remembered the parties where I was ignored when they found out I wasn't in show business or into drugs and had no important connections. Then there were the friends who tried so hard to make it in show business but never succeeded, sad and rejected.

Even the art world there was influenced by show business. I had met some of the artists in the top galleries, but there was no communication. In New York, that had been an important part of the art scene – discussing painting and what was happening in the galleries. The older artists we met in the Cedar Bar were always willing to discuss their work with students. At first I thought it was because I was a woman and didn't fit into the macho art scene in LA. But then I met an artist from South America, who was showing at the Museum. I was surprised to discover he had the same reaction when he was introduced to the LA artists.

I worked very much in isolation there, yet it was a good time to experiment and to find new directions in my work. Once a friend asked me to join a women's group called Women's Caucus for Art. I never liked women's groups, but feeling quite isolated as an artist in the vastness of LA, I decided to go to a meeting.

It was a "Pot Luck" at someone's home in Brentwood and I arrived with a casserole of yellow squash. I felt doomed from the onset. Someone asked me if I had used a food processor. In those days I didn't know what a food processor was, so I immediately revealed my limited cooking knowledge. Then someone asked if I was divorced and how many children I had. My negative answers placed me immediately as an outsider. As the evening wore on, the conversation seemed geared more to single mothers and women's liberation than art. I heard all about their bad experiences with men. I didn't dare mention Gregory who I was seeing at the time, so obviously I didn't have much to contribute to the conversation.

I went home feeling depressed, an outsider, a Green Monkey. I phoned Gregory to tell him about my disastrous evening with the Women's Caucus for Art. Before I got into it, he said he would like to apply for the role of Art. I told him he better think twice about it with these women. I went back to painting in isolation.

*   *   *

By now we were driving over the mountains north of San Bernardino into clear air with blue sky overhead. I felt I could breathe again. The nightmare of Los Angeles and Neil seemed further in the past than ever.

I had always wondered when and if I would find a "life" in LA. I had a few scattered friends in the hills, but nothing I could call a "life" – that meant feeling settled, having a good relationship, having intimate friends. My life had no cohesion. It was lonely, meaningless, unconnected, like LA itself.

Not long ago, I heard from an old boyfriend, Craig Daniels. He said he had been going through his address book and found my name (after ten years!). He was one of those good-looking, noncommital actors I had known who probably chose to see me as the dumb blonde. He was part Cherokee with high cheek bones and steel-grey hair. Who wouldn't be flattered by his attention?

Craig had reminisced about our lives in LA – walking his dog, Trump, on Malibu Beach, going to dinner parties I didn't remember and, oh yes, my wonderful little Spanish house that he had always loved. (It was safe to love a house.) He was retired now and living in New England, an idyllic setting where he could ride his bicycle along the coast. The romantic image sounded like J.B. Fletcher. It was nice to think of some connection to that period, even if it was as remote as Craig Daniels. I realized that we were never important to each other. I certainly had no interest in seeing this man again!

In contrast, my life seemed fuller now, interconnected with people. There was nothing permanent or settled, but we all related to different aspects of each other. Maybe living in a small town made the difference. I felt a part of the town. I realized I wasn't afraid of aloneness anymore. In fact, I really kind of enjoyed being alone after the years with Neil. Was I accepting the Green Monkey in me?

When I had read the essay about the Green Monkey, it said that the Green Monkey is an outsider, unconventional and some people are threatened by it. It's not inside the tribe! I'll always remember that therapy session when Byron told me about the Green Monkey, but at times I forget I'm a Green Monkey.

I ruminated over the thought that maybe all single women are Green Monkeys, or perhaps Purple Monkeys. After a few years of experiencing the world of couples, I now had to face the fact that I was back in the singles' world. A single woman at a dinner party made most married couples feel uneasy, whereas a single man was always a plus.

Even if I went to a party with an attractive date, I was still single and that was seen as threatening. There were a few exceptional friends who would invite me to dinner parties alone and compensate for my lack of a mate by inviting two gay men, which was really alright with me.

I had come to realize that my individual side was an asset. I was comfortable with my creative friends who didn't fit any mold, and I found the very conventional people (the sort who had rejected my mother) were often dull and uninteresting.

I went to my astrologer a few months ago. The most pertinent thing she told me was that my freedom was extremely important to me. I already knew that, but it was interesting to have it validated by my chart. She said I could never have been happy in a routine marriage and she saw lot of "unconventional" relationships. She was certainly right about that.

* * *

I opened my eyes just as we passed the sign for Victorville. I looked at Zane and thought: why couldn't I fall for a guy like him – he seems so rational? But there was no chemistry between us.

Zane had thought I was asleep. He commented, "I think we better have this truck serviced before we head out into the desert. I know there's a stretch ahead where there's nothing for about a hundred miles."

I agreed and then it suddenly dawned on me, "Zane, we never had lunch! All we ate today was that awful doughnut. I saw a Red Lobster as we drove in. That's probably as good as we can get here. How about a drink and dinner?"

He grinned, "Sounds pretty good to me." We found a Zip Lube that was still open and drove in to have everything checked on the truck. It seemed like an endless wait, but we were finally headed to the restaurant.

We walked into the Red Lobster after leaving the truck parked by a window. We didn't know whether Neil had alerted the State Police about a stolen truck, so we wanted to keep it in our sight.

As we drank martinis, we sat there just grinning wide grins at each other. Then we ravenously ate shrimp scampi, salad, cheese rolls and large baked potatoes with butter and sour cream. I looked at Zane and said, "I had no idea I was so hungry. It was the last thing on my mind today."

He said, "Mine too. Now I'm all set for the drive. Shall we go?"

CHAPTER TWENTY-NINE

It was about 6:30 P.M. when we started across the desert – a hot, balmy night with lots of vacationers on the road. Zane never said much about Neil, but he always spoke in a disparaging tone when his name came up. I wasn't sure what Zane thought of Neil, but I knew they often met in the morning at Downtown Subscription for a paper and coffee. I had thought they were good friends at one time, but Zane never seemed really surprised when I told him Neil had left.

When I called him for legal advice soon after Neil moved out, he was very willing to help me. He knew I was upset, but I was trying to be objective, reasonable, and all that to hide it, as I still considered him Neil's friend. He told me exactly what to do about the legalities I questioned.

Then to my surprise, he said not to mention that I had ever talked to him.

He had looked at me with that knowing grin he had and said, "I'm not surprised he's going back to LA. Santa Fe wasn't the right place for him. You know people say Santa Fe accepts or rejects you." There was a lot I could read into that. It was Zane's way of saying what he thought of Neil, and I knew he was my friend.

Reflecting on the whole experience, the good and bad, it had affected me in an unexpected way. I was more content with my life than I had been for a long time. I had learned a lot of things *not* to expect in a relationship. I also learned how important it was to have my own boundaries and to express my needs. What surprised me was that I wasn't sure I wanted to be with any man, though I had a much better idea of how to make a relationship work.

My astrologer had pointed out that it was essential for me to communicate, since my moon was in Gemini. She said, "the worst thing anyone could do to you would be to cut you off without discussing issues." I knew she was so right!

She had been the one who had brought up all the unconventional relationships in my chart. When had I ever had anything else? Neil had been my one serious attempt to make it work. Going way back, she said it was all because Venus was retrograde when I was born, which meant my creative energies were directed inward towards being an artist. At least it gave me *some* insight into my love life.

Zane must have been connecting with my thoughts about astrology as he looked toward the heavens and said, "Have you ever seen brighter stars up there? Boy, I've always loved the desert." I looked at the starry sky over the dark desert feeling like such a little speck on this earth, but a happy speck.

Zane looked tired and I suggested, "Why don't you let me drive for awhile. You could pull off at that exit and we could get out for a stretch." He pulled off the road and we stood in the vastness of the night with nothing much visible but the sky overhead, before we switched seats and took off again.

A dream I'd discussed with Byron came back to me now:

I'm dressed up, going to clubs with a group of friends in a new city in the desert. I lose the others so I go shopping with Carrie, a compulsive shopper who loves clothes. We try on hats, but they are too big.

Then we're at the airport on a bus going down the runway trying to catch a plane. We get on the plane and

209

I'm sitting right behind the pilots. One is a flustered woman who is complaining. I worry about her ability to fly the plane, but I draw back the curtain and see a male co-pilot sitting next to her. I feel better that he's flying it, too.

Byron pointed out that I'm close to the driver's seat supplanting my mother. I'm also looking for a new persona in the shopping, one that isn't tense and angry, a new consciousness in a new city. I was beginning to feel the change standing there in the desert.

About midnight, I passed the driving over to Zane. I could tell he was tired, too, and it was another half hour to Flagstaff, where we had planned to stop for the night. When we got to Williams, I suggested we look for a hotel. The first one was full, and the desk clerk said we would probably have to go on to Flagstaff. But I spotted a Ramada Inn on the left and pointing to it said, "Pull over. Let's try one more."

I fell out of the truck and rang a bell in the lobby a few times before an East Indian man in a nightshirt appeared. Anxiously I asked, "Do you have two rooms?"

"No, but I have a beautiful suite and I give you a special deal. There's a picture of it behind the desk." It looked big, complete with plastic flowers on the coffee table.

I went to the car to tell Zane I didn't mind sharing a room with him at this hour and sent him in to see the photo. He came out with the key and we parked behind the building out of sight.

There were two big beds. I immediately fell into one and I was asleep before Zane turned out the lights.

My dream was exceptionally clear and light:

I'm in a lovely, open beach house. There's a party going on and a girl invites me to go to the guest house to try on new dresses. They are sequined in bright colors with cutout silk stoles in odd shapes, but the dresses are terribly short, not what I would ordinarily wear. We go back to the house wearing the dresses, but the furniture is different and there's a new group of people. We don't know any of them, but it doesn't seem to matter.

The dream seemed like a positive omen for a new future. Suddenly a train went through the room blowing its whistle. I sat up, wide awake. The train was just outside the window, loud enough to wake anyone at six in the morning.

I lay down again with images of this new persona in a sequin dress running through my head. It seems like a positive change in this charming beach house with new people to meet. I felt in a good mood in spite of my exhaustion.

211

I heard a groan and Zane saying, "Are you awake?"

I glanced over at him. "Wide awake, I'm afraid! Do you want to get up?"

I took a shower. I wasn't really awake. Then we were on the road driving toward Flagstaff. The morning was grey with a slight drizzle and you couldn't see the mountains above Flagstaff. I just let Zane talk – something about using this whole adventure as a tax write-off.

He was feeling perky and rambled on "The first thing to do is put the truck in your name. Knowing Neil, he wouldn't hesitate to steal it back again."

I saw an exit sign with a number on it. I interrupted Zane saying, "Do you think that's an exit to Flagstaff?" We were already past it.

He looked back but said, "No, it's too soon." We'd only been driving about ten minutes. Flagstaff was about thirty miles, so I assumed he was right.

But as I looked behind us, I could see the mist lifting off the mountains "Zane, I think we missed Flagstaff!" It was like a time warp.

He looked back in surprise and commented, "I don't think we were meant to stop there." He grinned, "It just occurred to me – if there was a police report out on the truck and they thought we were heading for New Mexico, that's exactly where they would be looking for us."

"There's another town in about 40 miles where we can have breakfast," I said as I looked at the map.

The small town of Winslow had one long dusty street, and we found a place to have a delightfully greasy breakfast which fortified us for the day ahead.

Then we got back in the truck and raced on through the desert. We listened to a tape of Tony Hillerman's *Skinwalkers*, a mystery set in the Navajo country we were driving through. I leaned back realizing that I felt optimistic.

I see now that Neil was a big step forward for me in the whole process of change. I had learned a lot from the relationship. I was more open now, able to respond to others. If I didn't agree with someone, I could say no. I didn't have to be a caretaker, and if someone like Neil didn't like it, that was just too bad.

I had failed at making the relationship work, but I think that was attempting the impossible. It takes two to make a relationship and a lot of understanding. Without that, there's not a chance of being happy. I think Neil manipulated me into the person he needed, but then he lost sight of the real me and lost interest.

Failure is hard to admit. I remembered someone saying to me, "You can't succeed all of the time. If you win 70% of the time, that's very good." I used to think I had to win all the time, and I felt guilty or a loser if I didn't. This was like telling me I had the right to be human.

CHAPTER THIRTY

The day was hot and dry as we drove toward Santa Fe. My curiosity got the best of me and I hesitantly asked Zane about his girlfriend. She was very attractive and friendly, but remained a bit of a mystery to me.

He looked sheepish. Eventually he said, "You know, it's not a lot better than you and Neil – she's distant like Neil."

I said, "She seems very dependent on you, but I could never see the closeness."

He sighed, "You know, I don't think men really understand intimacy. When people want something from you, they aren't open and there's no trust. Oh, there's the attraction and attachments, but I don't know about closeness."

At least he was being honest. I said, "It always seemed such a simple thing to me. If you care about someone and talk honestly about your feelings, you would think anything could be resolved, but it's not that easy. People have hidden shadow sides – even you and me – that are unbelievably secret and threatening."

He nodded, "Maybe you're different, but when you get involved, there are always issues. Boy, I don't have any answers to it." He thought a moment and then decided to ask, "Have you read *Men are from Mars, Women are from Venus?*"

I said I had. "But," I commented, "even that is from a man's point of view. At least Gray points out that men and women are different, but he doesn't seem to get it! He says women don't want solutions to their problems, they simply want you to listen to them, agree with them and understand. That's not it."

Zane looked puzzled, "Well, then, what do they want?"

"Women want to find out what the other person thinks. That's how you communicate. Men don't know how to have a conversation. They want to tell you how it is. They have to prove they are right. For women, a discussion doesn't need to be right or wrong. The worst part is that men don't want to listen. They want to lecture you."

"Yeah, maybe, but aren't we talking about it now?"

"Yes, but you're stuck in a truck with me and we aren't in a relationship. You don't feel you have to compete, to win points or anything."

"I'll think about that." He laughed to himself.

He wasn't very reassuring and the conversation seemed to be at an end. Obviously he wasn't ready to get into a deeper discussion. I settled back to hear the second side of the Hillerman tape. There was a lot of flat dull country until we reached the red rocks at the New Mexican border. The day dragged on and it was late afternoon before we approached Albuquerque. After we stopped at the airport to pick up my car, I followed Zane on to Santa Fe. We were back in my world again. All that open space – you could see forever, and I breathed a sigh of relief as I drove out of the airport.

We had agreed to meet at Tim's house where we could hide the truck out among the pinons until I got it registered in my name. On the dirt road, we passed a truck heading out in a cloud of dust and all came to an abrupt stop. It was Tim. We asked him about hiding the truck behind his house. He looked puzzled, but said, "Fine. Just park it in the back." I'm sure he wondered why we were hiding the truck. We found a spot behind his portal where the truck wasn't visible from the road.

I realized how exhausted I felt as Zane drove me to my house. My cats looked at me as though I had returned from the dead and that's how I felt. I said to Sage, "It's only been two days," finding it hard to believe.

I slept until ten the next morning. Then I called Tim to explain about the truck. He said I'd better come out and he'd help me clean the truck before I put an ad in *The New Mexican* to sell it.

As we vacuumed the inside, I told him about the trip. He was intrigued by the fact that we went after the truck and laughed about our adventure. As we cleaned the windows, he said he missed doing these little jobs with Lita – one of the nice things about a relationship.

I agreed that it made a tedious job a lot more fun. (But it also made me realize that Neil seldom helped me with this kind of work and I had resented doing it alone.)

Before I left Tim invited me to a party the next evening, saying we both needed to meet some new people.

* * *

I came home to a long message on my answering machine from Liz. Was I back? Did we get the truck? I called her and we decided to meet for dinner at

"Celebrations," a restaurant on Canyon Road. The synchronicity of the name occurred to me as I entered the restaurant. What a perfect place to celebrate my success. I spotted Liz in the corner and waved.

Before I could say anything about the trip, Liz blurted out all her news. "Darling, I've found the answer. Have you heard of a book called *The Rules*?

I looked at her to see if she was serious. "Yes, but isn't that a bit juvenile…?"

But Liz ran on. "It works. The authors say that men want to do the pursuing. That's what it's all about. The chase. Once they have you, they lose interest. I've been using their advice on Harry. When he calls me, I don't call back for a few days. Then he gets anxious and sends a fax. You know how weeks would go by and I wouldn't hear from him? Well, now he calls me at least twice a week."

Harry was her wealthy, eighty-year-old lover who lived in New York with a much younger wife, but had never given up Liz. I could see the attraction, though I could understand why he never married her.

I finally said, "But, Liz, that's playing games. That's being deceitful and conniving and…"

"And they love it, my dear. It's not playing games. It's demanding respect, reconditioning the way they react to you."

I had to admit she had a very strong point, and it made a difference in their relationship.

We eventually got on the subject of my trip and she insisted on hearing all the details. She exclaimed, "I can't believe you found it so fast. God, am I glad I didn't go with you!" She was ecstatic about the whole story and ordered brandies after dinner to celebrate.

As I drove home, I began to see what she meant about *The Rules*. I had always been so accommodating. Maybe she was right as far as that went. But I still had a problem with pretense and games. That's not how I thought of a real relationship. Somewhere in the back of my mind, I hoped it was possible to be more honest with a man than she had been.

The phone rang as I walked into my house. As I picked it up I heard Nina's exasperated voice, "Where have you been? I've been trying to reach you for two days and I was beginning to get worried."

"I went to Los Angeles to get the truck."

"You what?"

"Well, I didn't go alone. Zane went with me and we stole it back from Neil."

There was a silence, then, "I don't believe it. You stole the truck?" I told her I would tell her every detail when I saw her, but that night I was too tired.

CHAPTER THIRTY-ONE

I was feeling good and yet I awoke the next morning out of a disturbing dream. It was time to call Byron, anyway, to tell him about the trip. Maybe it was the letdown after all the excitement, but why did I have this strange dream that seemed so dark? Byron said to come over that afternoon.

I wrote down the dream, pondering over its meaning. Later, after relating the whole saga to an amazed Byron, I related the dream to him:

I'm running through a slum, across a broken down porch toward the beach. I follow my old boyfriend, Craig, over sand dunes to the ocean. Then he disappears into the surf. I'm standing on a sand dune and, when some water comes in, the whole dune dissolves under me.

Later I go to a gallery that is representing my work. They show me enlarged photos of sculpture taken in public places.

I'm standing on the beach again and a huge sculpture appears in the ocean. It's not my work, but I can't seem to explain this to them.

The meaning of this dream wasn't at all clear to me. Nevertheless, Byron's face lit up, "You're losing the old structure. Who does Craig represent? The old dysfunctional male from your past and he's disappearing! The shadow aspect is dissolving!"

"Do you know what else is dissolving? My anger towards my mother. I don't blame her anymore! I needed to blame someone for my unhappiness. Now that I'm more aware of the whole drama, I don't need to blame anyone. She had her own problems that affected me, but I guess I can understand all of that now. It's sad that we could never be close, but in her own way, she gave me a lot."

"You're no longer as out of touch, not as isolated. Think of how withdrawn you were as a child. Remember the ski dreams: cold, high, isolated. The burden is lifted, it's not disturbing anymore. You're free, on the brink of departure. You can no longer be involved with the shadow men – the hidden. This is exciting! The unconscious is no longer a threat. Life can flow freely."

I said, "I knew there had to be something good in it because I wasn't depressed when I woke up. But what is that sculpture doing in the ocean?"

He answered enthusiastically, "That's even better. The sculpture surfacing in the ocean of the unconscious. It's what you've been working on all your life coming to fruition. The self is emerging."

There was another dream I wanted Byron to hear, as I hadn't seen him for a few weeks. This one seemed very optimistic to me:

I go to a party in Tesuque, a village near Santa Fe, to see a new house that is just finished. When I meet the architect, there's an immediate attraction. After we talk about houses, he tells me he wants to see me after the party.

I go home to feed the cat and return later. I look down at my feet, surprised to see I have on the old moccasins I wear for gardening. I decide it doesn't matter. I observe the house. There's a lot of open space, large windows and a living room with a ceiling rising up about sixty feet ending in a spire. I notice the bedrooms are downstairs. I've never liked going downstairs to bedrooms, but, otherwise, I think it's an exceptional house. The architect is tall with greying hair and seems rather serious.

Byron asked, "How does the dream feel to you?"

"It feels good — the house is a marvelous design, except for the downstairs bedrooms."

"Right, but the house has just been completed. I would call this a major resolution of the animus – a plateau, an arrival. Maybe this isn't the right design, not quite the right house yet – not quite the right man."

I agreed, "Yes, but he's a creative, successful man, a step in the right direction, I think."

"And this man wants to connect with you. He's light, he's not heavy, he's not intrusive. Not the heavy kind of animus you grew up with. The quality of light is good in the dream. This newly completed structure is almost church like…"

I add, "The spire is incredible!"

"Yes, it's as-spiration with the male. You want an evolved male. You don't want these idiots anymore."

"What did I see in them?"

Byron gave me that smug, all knowing look, "I'll tell you what you saw in them. The duty of your karma. You go through all these idiots in a lifetime to figure out enlightenment, to figure out the other side. It's about evolution and coming out with a spiritual animus, which is appropriate. You've just hit this level. He's not a madman. There are lots of possibilities."

"You didn't mention my moccasins." I said in a teasing way.

He smiled before making a serious observation, "Moccasins represent grounding, earth connection. You don't need to put on the dog. You're a connected woman, not plastic."

I left feeling elated, amazed at how the unconscious worked.

When I got home I felt more grounded than I could ever remember. Going through my mail, I found a letter from a gallery in Colorado saying they wanted to exhibit some of my paintings. I was thrilled. It was just what I needed to inspire me to get back to my easel. I had dealt with this Neil saga long enough and didn't need to dwell on it any longer. I wasn't depressed. I had images I wanted to paint. I was lucky to be an artist!

A relationship would have to wait until the right person came along, but I felt secure in my self and knew I could never be attracted to another Neil.

CHAPTER THIRTY-TWO

It occurred to me that I had a date with Tim later that afternoon. When we talked about going to the party, we had decided we would go to meet some new people. The drive took nearly an hour to the picnic on the Rio Grande near Taos. I was comfortable with Tim – no pretenses. He wasn't someone I needed to impress and his simple, down-to-earth manner was appealing.

When I got out of the truck I looked around at the people – mostly couples. I didn't see any single, attractive men. I sat down to talk with a couple I knew. Tim wasn't doing much better. I could overhear a conversation he was having behind me. A young woman asked, "Are you still practicing?"

There was a silence before Tim said, "I'm a sculptor. I practiced a long time ago, and now I'm working on large bronze sculptures." He sounded annoyed. There was a muffled apology as she realized he wasn't a lawyer. I tuned out in amusement.

Later I sat by him and asked if he had met any women he liked.

He sighed, "You know I think most of these women grew vertically to about five feet and then started going horizontal."

I laughed and said, "It's not a very interesting party, is it? I think meeting someone is up to fate and obviously there is no one here who has any karma with either of us."

As we walked to the truck, he smiled at me, "You know you look much better to me than any of the women here."

I responded, "And you're much more attractive than any of those men. More important, it's comfortable being with you."

He put his arm around me as we left. "I guess we'll just have to keep trying."

It felt good to have Tim as a friend. He had a sense of humor and we could laugh together. I realized that was all I wanted for the moment. I wasn't ready for a serious involvement yet.

* * *

The next day, it was time to deal with the truck again. I had made an appointment at the bank and I drove the truck down to Albuquerque. As I entered the basement office, all the women cheered. I couldn't believe the big welcome they gave me. I felt as though they were my allies. My guilt suddenly diminished.

They were curious about the friend who had retrieved the truck with me. Beth said, "If he ever wants a job repossessing cars, please have him call me."

I paid off the loan and thanked them. What a great relief! I hadn't realized that the whole issue of the truck had been hanging over my head for months, and now it was over. I no longer had any connection with Neil! Next stop was the DMV in Santa Fe and registering the truck in my name. I was having fun driving the little red pickup and looking down on all the cars.

* * *

It was a week before I had a call from Neil. When I heard his voice I was nervous, but acted surprised and cheerfully asked, "How are you?"

He responded, "Oh, fine, and how are you, darling?"

I said everything was going well.

Then he added, "Well, actually, there's a problem. The truck was stolen and the police haven't come up with any clues."

I guess I should have played along with it, but the game no longer intrigued me. I said, "No, Neil, it's not missing. I've got it."

There was silence, no reaction, no question about how "I got it." Then he asked where it was.

I explained how I had put the truck in my name and that I would be able to sell it without his signature. I could hear his voice sink. He must have realized there was no getting it back. But there were still no questions – play it cool, be charming. That was typical. We had a pleasant chat and I was glad to hang up. Fini!

EPILOGUE

The rest of the summer was uneventful. Zane broke up with his girlfriend and was taking a course called "Sex and Intimacy", which he found very enlightening. My painting was keeping me busy.

I continued to have dreams which I discussed with Byron. Two of those dreams seemed to be about completion:

I'm trying to find a place to park outside a hotel where I'm staying with a man, but I can't quite see him. The car dies and drifts down into a space. I call the garage where I bought it, but they no longer fix foreign cars. Another place I call can't repair it.

The man with me seems very remote and is no help. The owner of the hotel comes out and says he will help me

231

get the car fixed. He keeps appearing and seems to be a very stable person who can take care of everything. I notice that the owner is covered with a soft magnetic field and realize I'm very attracted to him.

We're staying in a beautiful suite with paneled doors and lots of mirrored walls. I hear a knock at the door and I know it's the owner. I open the door and he's looking up at a light that needs repairing. We stand very close and I touch him. He jumps back. I'm packing to leave, but I have a feeling the owner will appear again in my life.

Byron thought a moment, then he said, "I'm going to give this one a title: "The Reception of the True Animus". You recall your mother's psychotic animus, which we've been dealing with for so many years? Now we have the integration of the True Animus – this is the real stuff, the genuine article of safety, grounded, real….   This is a successful person who can fix things. You have all the lights coming on. This is the powerful archetype of repairing the light vehicle. Do you know why he jumps when you touch him?"

"I have no idea."

"You don't touch a god; look at what happens in the myths. You can't touch an archetype – it's too powerful, pure spirit, not of the earth. But just look at this. When you leave the shadow, you find the light. You're transforming the dark animus into the light one. The reward is contact, not abandonment."

"I felt so good after this dream!"

"You should. There's a lot of mirroring going on – facing one's own self, harmonious self-development that is appropriate at this point – in the real world."

I pointed out one thing to Byron, "It bothers me that the man, if he is my new animus, reminds me of my father, sort of a stable Ken Howard type."

Byron looked straight at me and said, "I'd say your father was pseudo stable – after all, he was married to your mother. Not stable underneath. Case closed."

I nodded, "I think you're right.

*   *   *

I had been to the Balloon Fiesta in Albuquerque that week. Hundreds of hot air balloons ascend at dawn and it's a spectacle worth getting up at 5:00 AM to see. I had a dream about flying in a balloon and didn't make much of it, but I told Byron about the dream anyway.

I'm flying in a balloon over a beautiful landscape. The sky is brilliant blue. We pass very low over a city and I don't know how the balloon misses the buildings. Finally it comes down and lands on a ship in the river where I get off.

233

To my surprise, Byron smiled and said, "Now this seems to be even more of a resolution!" He came up with a wonderful interpretation that hadn't occurred to me: "This is your conveyance to earth from high up. Wounded girls have to live up high. They get in trouble all the time because they aren't reality based. That's why they choose wounded men."

I responded, "You'd think they would find stable men, because they would feel so insecure."

"No, they pick the unstable ones, because that's all they know and that was your life. Look at the instability of both your parents. But now this tells me you're in harmony, resonance. You don't have to worry about the Neils anymore."

"No," I smiled, "I don't think I do."

"But the *dreams* tell me that, because you were very classic in your pain. It kept you from coming to earth. You never know where a balloon will go until it comes down to earth – they're very unpredictable. So you would select men who couldn't come to earth either. No one was less grounded than Neil or more unreal in his woundedness. And now you've landed – in the river of life! There's flow, no stagnation!"

He thought a moment, then added with a big grin, "And you land on a vessel in the river. A boat is an island of consciousness in the unconscious."

"So no more shadow figures in my life?"

"You know what I think? One of the purposes of this lifetime for you is to transform the shadow and bring it into the light, so you no longer have the pain of darkness, living in the shadow of unconscious people."

"I think so and I think I've arrived at that point."

Byron smiled, "You know you've learned to claim your power and become a more aware, strong individual, don't you?"

"Yes," I said, "and isn't that what we learn from the Green Monkey?"

He laughed and said, "I think you've got it."

I smiled at myself. We had come a long way. I guess I really was a Green Monkey. I also realized that I liked being a Green Monkey which had to mean that I liked my self.

THE END

Fredericka Heller

ABOUT THE AUTHOR

As a child, Fredericka Heller studied music with her mother, a professional musician, and later went on to art school in New York City. She has worked in numerous galleries and exhibited her paintings extensively.

Having spent much of her life dealing in abstract media, writing, as a concrete means of communication, became of great interest to her. It was after many years of Jungian dream therapy that the idea for *Out of the Shadow* emerged.

Printed in the United States
32093LVS00001B/7-57

9 781403 335975